A Question of Principle ✓

Elham was a rich, successful barrister, about to take Silk, Rickmore a poorly paid PRO with a local firm; they had nothing in common other than the fact that their wives were sisters. One night, after Penelope and he had dined with the Rickmores, Elham ran a man down in his car. The accident was unavoidable, but if the police questioned him they would also breathalyse him; his blood alcohol would be found over the limit, and he'd be charged with a criminal offence which could mean that his career would be ruined. He did not stop, but drove on, hoping to escape detection.

Later Rickmore learned enough to identify Elham as the driver of the hit-and-run car and this knowledge presented him with the agonizing question of where his loyalties lay—towards truth and justice, regardless of the nature of the victim, or towards the brother-in-law he did not like?

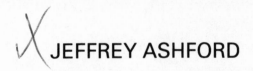

JEFFREY ASHFORD

A Question of Principle

COLLINS, 8 GRAFTON STREET, LONDON W1

William Collins Sons & Co. Ltd
London · Glasgow · Sydney · Auckland
Toronto · Johannesburg

First published 1986
© Jeffrey Ashford 1986

British Library Cataloguing in Publication Data

Ashford, Jeffrey
    A question of principle.—(Crime Club)
    I. Title
    823′.914[F]   PR6060.E43

ISBN 0 00 232078 9

Photoset in Linotron Baskerville by
Rowland Phototypesetting Ltd
Bury St Edmunds, Suffolk
Printed in Great Britain by
William Collins Sons & Co. Ltd, Glasgow

CHAPTER 1

The dining-room, which led directly off the kitchen, was small and the low, beamed ceiling and the wide, open fireplace made it seem even smaller still. There really was no room for the Elizabethan court cupboard, but this had come from Anne's home and she kept it because of the memories it held.

The four of them sat around the reproduction refectory table, Anne nearest the kitchen door. Elham brushed his lips with a serviette. 'That was a truly delicious piece of pork,' he said in his deep, fruity voice.

'Yes, wasn't it?' echoed Penelope. She turned to her sister. 'I just don't know how you learned to cook so well.'

'Necessity,' replied Anne, a touch of light irony in her voice.

'But Mother never taught us a thing. I mean, I simply wouldn't know where to begin.' 'Simply' was verbally underlined. She seldom spoke without underlining one word or another.

Rickmore had drunk enough not to guard his tongue as carefully as Anne would have had him do. 'If the need ever arises, no doubt you'll manage very successfully.'

'I don't think she needs to worry,' said Elham pompously.

An oblique reference, wondered Rickmore, amused, to the fact that Terence Elham was a man with credit while Dennis Rickmore was a man of credit—mortgage, overdraft, strained relations with the credit card firm . . .

'Let's clear the table, Dennis,' said Anne, 'and bring the sweet in.'

He looked briefly at her. There was a warning gleam in

her eyes. Don't start sniping at them. She was right, of course, but it was a pity not to pull the legs of two people who were so self-satisfied that they seldom realized their legs were being pulled. He stood, saw that Elham's glass was empty and picked up the bottle of wine. He went round the table to top up Penelope's glass.

She put her hand over the rim. 'Not for me, thanks. I'm on cloud nine already.'

More affectation? She seemed totally unaffected by what she'd drunk. Or were the effects merely well camouflaged? Anne had told him that Penelope was drinking heavily nowadays and always had a couple of vodkas before going out to a party in case the hospitality was poor. She claimed that vodka wasn't really alcoholic, not like gin or whisky. She had the useful ability of being able to believe whatever it suited her to believe.

'Come on back to earth,' said Anne.

He refilled Elham's glass.

'The Spaniards,' said Elham, 'seem to be improving the quality of their wine these days.'

'They are. You ought to try all the different Riojas one can buy now.'

'I most certainly will.'

He most certainly wouldn't, thought Rickmore. He emptied the bottle into his own glass after Anne had shaken her head to show she didn't want any more. It wasn't smart to drink Spanish wine; French, of course, German provided it didn't contain too much anti-freeze, and Californian if one were slightly eccentric. He raised his own glass and drank. Bad manners to drink standing up. It was fun confirming their opinion of him . . . He checked his thoughts, vaguely astonished to discover that they were becoming slightly incoherent. He carried the now empty bottle and the meat dish through to the kitchen.

The kitchen, part of the outshut, was very small and there

was little working surface; what there was, was now crowded
with the bowls, dishes and utensils, used in the cooking and
preparation of the meal. He stood in the centre, his head
only an inch beneath the ceiling. 'Where . . . where shall I
put the meat dish?'

Anne, her dark blue eyes expressing amusement, murmured: 'You, sir, are half sloshed!'

'Absolute nonsense.'

'Repeat after me, I've sipped solely a sustaining suffici-
ency, certainly insufficient to succour a social solecism.'

'Like hell!'

'Probably very wise of you.' She moved a mixing bowl
and then took the meat dish from him and put it down.

'You wrong me.' Even when completely sober, he occasionally mispronounced his R's.

'I doubt it.'

'Very well. I will prove I can speak in many tongues. I
see . . . I saw sea shells . . .'

'If I were you, love, I'd look some other time, when the
sea's not quite so choppy . . . The pud's in the fridge, along
with cream. Are you up to whipping that?'

'Any more cheek and I'll show you exactly what I am up
to whipping.' He went across to the refrigerator and, very
carefully, brought out four individual bowls of chocolate
orange mousse, putting each one on top in turn. 'Where's
the . . . the cream?'

'In front of your nose.'

He lifted out the carton, shut the refrigerator door—a
little more enthusiastically than he'd intended—moved over
to the food mixer.

'Dennis, you know that's not working.'

He remembered.

'Use the beater.'

He poured the cream into a plastic bowl and whisked it,
bothered for most of the time by the bowl's tendency to crab

sideways. When the cream held a point, he tapped the whisk to clear it, then began to walk over to the doorway.

'Are you thinking of serving the cream in that bowl?'

He looked down and was immediately amused by the thought of his sister-in-law's and brother-in-law's expressions at the sight of whipped cream being served in a kitchen bowl . . . He corrected his thoughts. Terence was a man of precision. So it was sister-in-law and sister-in-law's husband . . .

'For heaven's sake, wake up. Here, give it to me.'

He handed her the bowl. 'I'll get the white wine.'

'Don't you think . . .' She stopped. They didn't drink wine very often and it seemed a pity to suggest he left the third bottle unopened merely because he'd obviously had enough. Since the pre-dinner drinks, some of the lines had disappeared from his face and his manner had become light and ironic, reminding her of when they'd first known each other and the world had been all sunshine . . . She sighed as she opened the cupboard to the right of the sink and brought out the small silver dish, another legacy from her parents' home. Normally, other people's prosperity was no cross to bear, but when those other people were close relations who made a point of underlining their prosperity . . . There was laughter from the dining-room. Had Dennis been misguided enough to tell them about the judge who stuttered? If so, Terence's laughter had been very false. For him, the law was not a subject about which one joked . . .

'Not your chocolate orange mousse?' said Penelope, as Anne walked through the doorway, carrying a tray with the four glass bowls and the cream on it. 'Didn't I say before we left home, Terence, that we'd have the most perfect meal?'

'You most certainly did.'

'Much nicer than if we'd gone to the Gordons' . . .' She stopped abruptly.

'What's this?' asked Rickmore. 'It sounds to me, Penny, as if you had a second invitation for tonight.'

'Well, we . . .' She looked at her husband.

'As a matter of fact, we did,' said Elham, now at his most urbane. 'But since we didn't receive it until after yours, and since we'd no doubts about which one we'd rather accept, we naturally refused the Gordons.'

'We're flattered.' Even Rickmore accepted that this was a moment to keep quiet, but the wine was too lively for him to do so. 'And very highly honoured!' Never let it be forgotten that Sir Francis was a high court judge and therefore an invitation from him was to be regarded in the light of a royal command. So could Terence, a man who knew the value of every relationship (but the price of none), have willingly turned down this invitation? Surely not. Penelope must have persuaded him that they could not go back on their prior acceptance. Although every bit as much of a snob as he, she did make a point of honouring family ties . . .

Penelope, aware that there was a danger of something being said that could not easily be laughed off, changed the conversation and talked about a cocktail party to which she and Elham had recently been. Her remarks were amusing and only slightly catty.

Think what you like about her, Rickmore decided, as he poured out the white wine, you had to admit that her social skills were second to none.

The sitting-room was on the far side of the massive central chimney about which the house had been built. Like all the other rooms in the house, it was heavily beamed and the central one was deep so that anyone with any height had to duck to pass under it unscathed. Roughly square, the room had a single small window and was naturally rather dark. A modern fireplace had been built within the very wide inglenook one and although from any æsthetic point of view this should have been ripped out, since it gave out so much more heat than the original would have done, it had been left. As Anne had once said, it was much easier to be an æsthete when one was well off.

Rickmore got up from one of the armchairs, crossed to the fire and threw on a couple of split logs; there was a rush of flame which caused a patch of soot to sparkle briefly as it caught fire. He turned. 'How about the other half?'

'No more for me,' said Penelope. 'One more drop of alcohol and I'll be seeing quadruple.'

'You'll be seeing what?' Elham, who'd begun to slump in the armchair, jerked himself upright. 'What did you say, Penelope?'

'I said I can't possibly drink any more or I'll be seeing quadruple.'

'Nonsense. Do think before you speak.'

'But you're always saying that thinking is dangerous for me.'

'You're talking ridiculously.'

She was hurt by his bad-tempered words.

Rickmore said: 'You'll join me in another brandy, won't you, Terence, even if the girls have chickened out?'

'But we brought it as a present for you,' protested Penelope, 'not for us to drink.'

'A present shared is a pleasure doubled.'

'What a marvellous sentiment. I just can't think how you can be so clever as to think up something like that.'

Anne said drily: 'He adapts the original.'

Rickmore made a face at her. 'Can't you leave any illusions in other people's minds?'

'Don't you mean delusions?'

He laughed, went over to the small mother-of-pearl inlaid table and picked up the bottle of Martell VSOP the Elhams had brought. 'You didn't get the chance to answer me, Terence. Will you have another snifter?'

'Snifter?' replied Elham. 'It's a long time since I've heard that expression.'

'I'm firmly rooted in the past.' He collected Elham's glass, poured into it a very generous measure, returned it. He collected his own glass and helped himself equally liberally. When he sat, he did so much more heavily than he'd intended and a little cognac slopped over the edge of the glass. He licked his hand. 'As my mother always taught me, waste not, want not.'

Elham sententiously thought it was a pity that Rickmore's mother hadn't also taught him that a gentleman did not lick his hand in public.

It was a clear night and the sky was alive with stars; the rising moon was beginning to cast vague shadows. In the distance, a vixen began to cry, in reality calling for a mate, but sounding as if in agonized torment; much nearer, a roosting pigeon was disturbed and the clap of its wings carried far.

Penelope passed through the outside doorway of the porch, then turned. 'It's become very much colder,' she said, from within the comfort of her full-length silver fox coat. 'Don't stand there with the door open, go on back into the warmth.'

'You're right, it is colder,' said Anne, 'so I think I will.'

Penelope stepped forward to embrace her sister and kissed her on both cheeks. 'It's been an absolutely perfect evening. I haven't enjoyed one so much in years and years.'

'Good.' Anne freed herself.

'Good night, Anne,' said Elham. 'The meal was truly delicious.' From their first meeting, he had correctly judged that, in direct contrast to her sister, she eschewed all affectation and he never made the mistake of showing her more than genuine respect. This respect occasionally made him wonder why she'd married Rickmore. With her attractive looks and warm personality, her reasonable and logical approach to everything, and her determination, she surely could have found a husband with a much sounder financial background.

Anne said one last good night and then closed the outside door of the porch; since it was glass, light continued to spill out on to the brick path to help them until they came within range of the outside light on the corner of the house.

Elham's dark green Jaguar was parked outside the garage —a World War Two army hut which was beginning to look as if it dated back to World War One. The Jaguar was an XJ-S, breathed upon and customized by Steerson; the V12 engine had been developed to produce 340 bhp, the suspension had been modified to accept this extra power, and the interior was even more luxurious than was that of the standard model. It was impossible to mistake the fact that this was a rich man's car.

'How's it going?' asked Rickmore.

'As smooth as silk,' replied Elham, with deep satisfaction.

'From what I've read, the engine is built like a Swiss jeweller's watch.'

'I wouldn't know how it's built; only how it goes.' He went to pull out the keys from his pocket and was surprised to discover how clumsy his fingers had suddenly become.

'She does use rather a lot of petrol, though?'

He shrugged his shoulders. He couldn't be expected to concern himself about that; if a man had to worry about the fuel consumption, he had no business buying the car. He finally managed to bring out the keys and went to insert one in the lock of the door; somehow he missed and the point of the key briefly scraped along the paintwork. He swore, conscious he was making a bit of a fool of himself. He tried again and this time the key went home. He turned it and the four doors unlocked. He pulled open the door and

Penelope, after kissing Rickmore on both cheeks, climbed in and sat.

Elham went round to the driver's door. 'Thanks again, Dennis.'

'It's been a pleasure.'

But for whom? he wondered as he settled behind the wheel. He started the engine and then blipped it, unable to resist the satisfaction of showing how much power lay under his command. Then he engaged Drive, released the hand-brake, and accelerated.

The drive, perhaps more accurately described as a slightly upmarket yard, ended at wooden gates which were always left open; in the headlights, the broken bottom crosspiece of one of them was obvious. Rundown, like so much about the place, he thought. As they turned left on to the road, there was a muted squeal from the tyres. He was vaguely surprised to discover that they'd been travelling that quickly.

The slightly undulating road ended at a T-junction. He turned right, came to a halt at crossroads fifty yards further on. On their right was a pub. Rickmore had said that occasionally he went in there and had a drink. A typically pointless exercise since only the local yokels would use it— but his brother-in-law had no grasp of priorities.

The road was clear and he accelerated, fiercely enough momentarily to pin them back in their seats.

'Don't drive so fast,' she said petulantly.

'You call that fast?' He laughed. When he'd been young . . . He corrected his thoughts, which had been about to indulge in fantasy. When he'd been young, he hadn't owned a Jaguar and burned up the roads. He hadn't even owned a clapped-out Mini. He could still remember the scorn of a girl he'd met at a bottle party when he'd confessed to being carless. She'd turned down a suggestion of another meeting. That, surely, had been some time during his pupillage, when every penny had had to be made to do the work of four . . .

'For God's sake, Terence, slow down and keep to your side of the road.'

'Stop fussing,' he snapped. It was generally supposed by their friends that she couldn't be as vacuous as she appeared and that therefore it was all a pose. But the pose was that she couldn't. But she was beautiful and when he saw the envy and desire in other men's eyes, he was content, except . . .

'Do look what you're doing.' Her voice was now shrill.

He steered for the nearside as he stamped on the brakes. The car skidded very slightly on the damp road, but then corrected itself without any action on his part; indeed, he didn't even become aware that they had begun to skid until it was all over.

Despite his braking, they still entered the left-hand corner too fast, especially remembering that there was a sharper right-hander a hundred yards further on. He was considering the need to brake again—and to return to the left-hand side of the road—when from a rough copse on their right a man ran out. Elham swung the wheel to the left, but the off-side wing hit the man and sent him flying, a Catherine wheel of arms and legs.

CHAPTER 2

Elham braked as he looked up at the rear-view mirror. The soft moonlight was just strong enough for him to be able to make out the dark bundle in the middle of the road. He tried to assure himself that it was moving.

'What are you doing?' she demanded shrilly. 'You fool, don't stop.'

'But . . .'

She gripped his shoulder and shook it, careless of what effect this had on his driving. 'For God's sake, keep going.'

'He may be hurt,' he mumbled.

'Someone else can cope.'

The car had slowed to little more than a walking pace. He half-turned and looked at her as he desperately tried to force his mind into focus. 'But I daren't just drive on. The law . . .'

Her voice rose still higher. 'Can't you understand? If you report it, they'll breathalyse you.'

He realized that she was right. It wouldn't matter that the accident had not been his fault, that the man had run into the car rather than that the car had hit him. They would insist on checking his blood/alcohol level and they'd find it was over the limit. From that moment on, it would prove impossible to maintain that the collision had been unavoidable because insobriety raised a presumption of guilt which was almost impossible to rebut . . . So if he stopped now, he must inevitably end up by being charged . . .

The Bar was jealous of its reputation and demanded that those who practised at it were beyond criticism. To be found guilty of any criminal offence was likely to lead to disbarment; to be found guilty of a serious one inevitably did. So disaster lay ahead. And this at a time when he had applied for Silk and his future seemed set to attain heights which thirty years ago had appeared unrealistic day-dreams . . .

His mind was trained to cut through confusion and to recognize essentials and now, despite the acohol, despite the shock and panic, he understood that disaster need not lie ahead if only he could conceal his part in the accident. Could he?

Hit-and-run cases presented the police with difficult investigations and their clear-up rate was not high. Usually, they only solved them when someone was able to give an initial indication of the vehicle's identity—only then could they call in experts to make the necessary positive identification. This initial indication normally came from one of three sources—an eyewitness (who might be the victim), the sighting of a vehicle damaged in a manner consistent with the accident, or as a consequence of a report from the garage called upon to repair such damage (ironically, requested in an attempt to conceal it). Here, there had been no eyewitness other than the victim. He had run out from the copse so carelessly that it was impossible to believe he could have taken any notice of the approaching car through the glare of the headlights. After the impact, shock must surely have prevented accurate observation? So if he drove on now, the odds were heavily against the victim being able to give the police any useful evidence. And once back at Popham House, he could check the damage the car had suffered and decide what steps needed to be taken to conceal it . . .

Although this was never a busy road, there was bound to be another vehicle along fairly soon, so the injured man would not be long without help . . .

He accelerated. They rounded the right-hander and drew level with the cricket pitch, fenced off from the sheep which grazed the outfield during the winter. Ahead of them, another vehicle approached, its headlights picking out the pollard willows which lined the stream which separated the road from the field. He realized that if he'd hesitated even a few more seconds, he'd have been unable to escape disaster and he felt sick at the thought.

'I do believe that Terence is getting even more pompous,' Rickmore said, as he used a pair of tongs to lift a partly burned log to one side of the fireplace.

'What lies behind that observation—sour grapes?' asked Anne.

He put the tongs back on the stand, picked up the fire-guard and set it in front of the fireplace. As he stood upright, he said: 'You really think that?'

She regarded him for several seconds, then answered as she ran her fingers through her thick curly black hair which refused to be constrained or styled and had filled her with despair until she had learned to leave it to grow as it demanded. 'Not in the sense that you envy him his possessions. But maybe yes in the sense that you envy him the security that those possessions give him.'

'I suppose I have to admit I'd like to be able to forget the more mundane problems of life, such as how can we afford to live next week.'

'We always manage.'

'But I can't buy you all the new clothes you need . . .'

'If you're thinking of that silver fox, forget it.'

'The what?'

'Wasn't it Penny's new coat which made you say that?'

'I didn't realize it was new—I thought it was the old one.'

She laughed as she came forward and rested her forearms on his shoulders and linked her fingers behind his head. 'If she knew that you never realized she was wearing a brand new silver fox coat, she'd be spitting six-inch nails.'

'I'm just dead unobservant and ignorant.'

'When it comes to fur coats, undoubtedly.' She kissed him. 'That's one of your attractions.'

'Then you're prepared to admit I do have some?'

She kissed him again, then released him and stepped back. 'You know what I think of fishing for compliments?'

'The bait's never right?'

'The fish you catch are rotten . . . Come on, instead of talking nonsense, let's go to bed.'

'Right,' he said with enthusiasm.

'You've had too much to drink to think along those lines; aren't you remembering your Shakespeare?'

'At this time of night? Anyway, didn't he also say that he always hath a way?'

She knew a warm happiness that she was married to a man who could talk stupidities instead of stocks and shares and futures. She yawned. 'I thought that pud I made was quite nice.'

'So now who's fishing?'

'All right, I am. So you can damn well tell me what you thought of my chocolate orange mousse.'

'Lumpy.'

She whirled round, picked up a cushion from the settee, and hurled it at him. He ducked and the cushion swept across the top of a small occasional table, sending objects flying. 'Damn!' she exclaimed.

'No doubt you expect me to apologize for ducking?'

'Of course.' She went over and knelt, to discover exactly what, if any, damage she'd caused. The chased silver snuff-box was undented. 'That's all right, thank goodness . . . I do wonder what's happened to Uncle Paul? It's strange to have a blood relative who took off from home and hasn't been seen or heard from since.'

'One day he'll turn up, looking for his favourite niece because he wants to leave her all those vulgar oil wells he owns back in Texas.'

'When I was young, I used to have that kind of daydream. But when I mentioned it to Mother, she said that Paul would only reappear if he were broke.' She returned the snuffbox to the table. 'He gave me this two days before he disappeared. I often wonder why he did.'

'Perhaps he thought he was about to snuff it.'

'God, your sense of humour doesn't improve! . . . What's this? Blast!'

'Now what's the matter?'

In answer, she held up a blue spectacle case.

'Are they Terence's?'

'Can't be anyone else's, can they? And he's bound to need them tomorrow, so he'll have to come back now and fetch them. Ring him up, will you, while I finish tidying up?'

He went through to the hall—like the kitchen, originally part of the outshut—and across to the corner cupboard by the doorway into the kitchen. He lifted the receiver off the telephone and dialled. The call was unanswered. 'They can't be back yet.'

She stood in the doorway of the sitting-room and looked at her watch. 'It's nearly twenty minutes since they left here. They must be back by now if they went straight there.'

'They're not likely to have done anything else at this time of night—Terence reckons that a late night leads straight along the path of unrighteousness.'

She thought for a moment, her features slightly blurred by the combination of light and shadow which softened them and added a touch of beauty to a face which normally held too much character to be termed beautiful. 'Try again.'

He dialled and there was still no answer.

'D'you think something's happened to them on the way back?'

'Very unlikely. The devil always looks after his own.'

'But they couldn't possibly take more than a quarter of an hour . . . I think I'd better drive over to see if they're all right and to return the glasses.'

'Why can't we just leave it . . .'

'Because we can't.'

'They would, if the roles were reversed.' He sighed. 'I know, they aren't.'

'That's not very fair.'

'Facts often aren't.'

'Now who's being pompous?'

'The final insult! OK, OK, I'll drive his spectacles back so that in the morning he can appear in court with his usual brilliance.'

'Are you sure you're up to driving?'

'I'm as sober as a judge.'

'Then heaven help justice . . . Darling, please go carefully.'

'On tiptoe, fairy-like . . . On second thoughts, not a very safe expression in this gay day and age.'

'Don't worry, you'll never be mistaken for one of them.' She returned to the sitting-room, brought back the spectacle case which she handed to him. 'Don't stay on for a nightcap, or anything.'

'Not a dram shall pass my lips. And as far as the anything is concerned, Penelope has never bewitched me while Circe weaves.'

'Idiot! Sometimes I think you're certifiable.'

'But charming.'

'God, you don't dislike yourself!'

'What cause have I ever had to? . . . I'll be back in a rush.'

'Just go and return at a sober pace.'

'Is our old banger capable of any other?'

He left the hall and went through the small porch to the outside. He was about to shut the porch door, when she called out: 'What about a coat?'

'Don't need one,' he replied, forgetting how cold it had become.

He walked along the brick path, round the corner of the house. He was, he thought as he opened the wooden gate, a very lucky man to be married to Anne. Life would be perfect if only he could earn a bit more money . . . It was funny how life usually made certain there was an if. Take Elham. He had success, money, and a very beautiful wife. Yet it had become clear in only the last few days that his life might hold an if. The previous Tuesday, over a drink in the Reckton squash club, Hugo Beeston had over-casually mentioned seeing Elham in a restaurant just off the Fulham Road, lunching with a sculptor who'd created a hullabaloo with her work. Beeston, a born gossip, had obviously been fishing for information as to whether the relationship was possibly more than a casual one. He'd gone away empty-handed. But could Elham be having an affair with a sculptor who was, apparently, noted for depicting the male member in unusual guises? It was a delightful thought . . .

He reached the garage, opened the right-hand set of doors and clipped them back. He didn't bother to switch on the light, but edged his way between the workbench and the Escort to the driving door. He settled behind the wheel, turned the key, and the engine churned over but did not fire. He tried again, with the same result. He remembered how the Jaguar had fired immediately and how the exhausts had burbled with the tenor of a running brook which might, at whim, be transformed into a raging torrent. When Anne had said that perhaps he envied Elham his sense of security, but not his material possessions, she'd forgotten that customized XJ-S.

The Escort's engine finally fired; the engine ran lumpily. Only recently, the garage had said that he couldn't expect much from a car which had been right round the clock once and seemed to be heading for its second century. He needed a new car. They hadn't added where he was to find the money to buy this new car.

He backed out, turned, drove on to the road and turned left to go down to the T-junction. Seven minutes later he approached the left-hand corner just before the cricket field to find that traffic cones had been set up on the road, together with a police notice to slow. Round the bend were parked two cars. Clearly, there had been an accident. He slowed down to a crawl, suddenly very conscious of the fact that he had drunk more than enough to be driving.

A policeman in uniform, reflector tabs on his sleeves and a reflective lollipop in his right hand, waved him on, his quick movements suggesting impatience. Probably, Rickmore thought, some of the passers-by had tried to rubberneck. He dropped down to second gear, hugged the left-hand verge, and drove past the policeman. He was aware of a group of people, but could not make out what they were doing. He reached the right-hander and passed a policeman who was ready to slow traffic coming in the opposite direction. By the time he was through the corner, all signs of the accident were gone from the rear-view mirror.

The road, turning this way and that for no obvious reason —the course of the rolling English drunkard?—crossed the tributary of the Wort and then climbed up over the railway line and into the village of Ailsham, a haphazard collection of centuries-old cottages, a few ugly modern council houses, a general store, and a pub. Beyond the village the road forked and he turned left.

Popham House lay a mile outside the village. Originally a typical farmhouse, probably built for a yeoman farmer of some consequence, with high-pitched roof, peg tiles, bricks made from clay dug nearby, and beams cut out from locally felled oaks, it had been enlarged and modernized by previous owners. Since they had had considerable taste and sympathy for period, the result had not been noticeably incongruous or anachronistic. Lacking such constraining influences, the Elhams had, when in turn they'd decided to have the enlarged house enlarged, demanded size and luxury irrespective of any other standards. Popham House was now the home of wealthy people who wanted others to admire and envy.

The large, fussily designed wrought-iron gates were open. So they had returned, thought Rickmore. Then why hadn't they closed them? Was Elham tighter than he'd seemed?

He drove through the gateway and into the macadamed drive. To the left was a three-car garage. The Jaguar was parked outside and Penelope and Elham were standing by it. Elham had a torch in his hand and this was switched on even though the outside lights on the garage were also on. As the Escort came to a stop, Rickmore was momentarily struck by the expression on their faces; it looked like fear, but since this must be an absurd flight of fancy, he dismissed the idea.

He opened the door, climbed out, and approached them. 'We tried to phone, but there wasn't any answer.'

They said nothing, but continued to stare at him. 'Is something wrong?' he asked.

'No,' Elham mumbled.

'You forgot your specs and we reckoned that as you'd need them tomorrow, I'd better run them over.'

'What . . . what's that?'

'Your spectacles—I've brought them.' He held out the case.

Elham took it and then there was a silence, which Rickmore finally broke. 'I'll be getting back home, then.'

Penelope made an effort to behave normally. 'Thank you so very much for bringing them. It's wonderfully kind of you.'

Despite their previous denial, Rickmore thought, they were behaving as if something were very wrong. But obviously they didn't want to discuss what that something was. He began to turn away when a brief fleck of light drew his attention to the offside wing of the Jaguar. He saw that there was a slight dent in it. Then his gaze moved down and, thanks to the angle at which he stood, he could just see that the offside light pod was smashed. Obviously Elham, his judgement affected by drink, had bumped into something as he drove in. No wonder the atmosphere was strained! And ten to one Penelope, whose second name was not discretion, had not had the sense to keep her opinions to herself . . .

Rickmore returned to the Escort and left.

Anne was in bed, the duvet drawn up half over her head as she often liked it—squirrelling warm, she called it. 'Was he grateful?' she asked sleepily.

'I wouldn't know.'

'What d'you mean?'

'When I arrived, both of them were still outside, standing around the Jag and staring down at a dent in one wing and a smashed headlamp.' He chuckled. 'For once, Terence's driving obviously wasn't up to genius standard.'

'Why's that so amusing? You have a mean sense of humour.'

'Like as not,' he replied complacently.

CHAPTER 3

Detective-Sergeant Ridley read through the brief typewritten report. At 11.17 the previous night, a man driving from Reckton to his home in Ackley Cross had come across a body lying in the road just past Ailsham cricket ground. He'd telephoned for help from the nearest house and the ambulance had arrived at 11.39, a couple of minutes after the first patrol car. The victim had suffered a hit-and-run accident. He had been taken to the Latimer General Hospital in Reckton, where his condition had been diagnosed as serious; he had a broken arm and two crushed ribs, but his main injury was a fractured skull and internal cranial bleeding. No prognosis had yet been given. Patrol car Tango Bravo Seven had gone to the hospital and PC Fielding had tried to identify the victim, but without success.

At the conclusion of the report was the usual compressed

description. Name, unknown; sex, male; colour, white; nationality, unknown; occupation, unknown; age, between 20 and 30; height, about 5ft 11ins; weight, about 160 lbs; build, medium; complexion, fair, freckles on cheeks; hair, brown, straight, bottle-brush style; eyes, small iris, light brown; eyebrows, arched, thin; nose, straight, very narrow saddle; face, long, clean-shaven; chin, square, dimpled; lips, thick, upturned corners; mouth, large; ears, large, close to head; forehead, slightly receding; distinguishing marks, tattoo 'BA' on right forearm; clothes (all without makers' tabs), black wool sweater, green shirt, navy blue jeans, vest, pants, socks, woollen gloves, plimsolls; jewellery, gold ring, plain, left middle finger; habits, heavy smoker, no sign of drugs. No papers. Prints taken and sent on.

He dropped the single sheet of paper on to the desk, yawned, ran the fingers of his right hand through his wavy brown hair. He lit a cigarette, looked at his watch. Five minutes to reporting to the DI.

Elham entered the first-class carriage and settled in the only vacant corner seat. ''Morning,' said Templeton, from immediately opposite. He nodded in reply. Templeton resumed reading his newspaper. Their conversation seldom went beyond this briefest of greetings. The train started and quickly gathered speed and soon they were rattling over the complicated system of points by the large marshalling yard which was used by passenger trains. Beyond this, the countryside stretched out, bare and dedraggled from the recent heavy rain.

Normally, Elham opened *The Times* at the law reports, studied these and agreed or disagreed with the decisions reached; then he spent the rest of the hour's journey learning what new mess the politicians had led the country into. Today, however, he left the newspaper unopened and stared out of the window. As the telegraph poles flicked by and the carriage rocked steadily, without any audible rhythmic accompaniment since here the line was continuously welded, he suffered a growing sense of resentment which, for the moment, even subdued his fears. There had been no need for Penelope to become so aggressively—and contemptuously?—commanding. He'd been shocked, of course, but he had not lost his wits. Why had she treated him like a child and spelled everything out? He'd appreciated the situation just as well as she. Given a little more time, he'd have done all that it was necessary to do. He'd always worn the trousers in their household and he'd no intention of handing them over now . . . This morning, when he'd said he was feeling too rotten to go to chambers, she could have shown sympathy instead of sarcastically asking if he really wanted people to wonder why he hadn't gone to work on the morning following the accident . . .

The train flashed through a small station so quickly that it was quite impossible to read the name; he didn't have to read it to know where it was because he'd been born four miles away—in a small, dingy semi-detached, one of a row of ten, inhabited by women who walked around in public in carpet slippers with curlers in their hair and men who sat down to meals in their braces. People born in such streets usually only left them in their coffins. But he'd had the drive and ambition to claw his way up and out into a different world and that was something Penelope shouldn't ever forget . . .

When he'd first met her, she'd had a circle of admirers, how large a circle and how admiring he'd been careful never to determine. But by then he'd discovered self-confidence —some might have described it as arrogance—and he had decided to marry her even though he was considerably older than she and totally lacking in the feckless, to-hell-with-tomorrow attitude towards life that her other male friends had possessed and which, in their stupidity, they'd considered one of the charms of their gilded circle. His self-confidence had been well founded. He'd had something to offer which none of them had: a glittering future . . .

Such reminiscences, with their underlying theme of self-approval, had the effect of lessening his resentment. And as it lessened, so his fears returned. What were the police doing at that moment? Searching the road and the grass verge for anything that would help lead to the identification of the hit-and-run car? The fleck of paint which could be matched with the paint from the suspect car (every car manufacturer cooperated with the police and sent in samples of the paints they used; the exact composition of the layers of anti-rust, undercoat, and topcoat, could identify the model); the sliver of glass from the headlamp which could be matched with the remaining glass; the tyre impression which could some-times be nearly as damning as a fingerprint; the pellet of mud, knocked off from the underside of the wheel-arch, which possessed peculiar characteristics and so identified an area where the car had been? . . . Certainly the police would have already circularized all garages and repair shops, asking to be informed if any car were brought in with damage that was consistent with its having hit a body . . . He'd explained all this the previous night, after the third whisky, when the horror of what had happened had gripped his lungs until he'd had difficulty in breathing. He'd said that running away hadn't solved anything because there was that dent in the offside wing of the Jaguar, together with the broken glass of the headlamp pod, and they didn't dare leave them as they were for fear of their being seen by a patrolling constable, and they didn't dare try to have them repaired because if they did then a report would be made to the police . . . He could still 'hear' the scorn with which she'd said that he was supposed to be the one with the brains, so hadn't he realized that the safest place in which to hide something was in full view? So all he had to do was drive the Jaguar into the corner of the garage, making certain that he caused enough further damage to erase all previous signs . . . He'd stared at her, slack-jawed, wondering how in the hell she, of all people, could have come up with the solution? And an answer had come to him. She had realized that the whole of her way of life was at stake and so she was fighting to preserve it with all the ferocity and ingenuity of a mother defending her young . . .

It was drizzling when they arrived at Cannon Street. He took a taxi to chambers and when he paid the fare and added to this his precisely calculated tip, the driver showed his contempt for such parsimony.

Haldane Buildings had originally been a large Edwardian block with four floors. During the war it had suffered some bomb damage which had left the top floor untenantable and as soon as possible after the war the block had been demolished and in its place a more elegant building, in Georgian style, had been erected, with much better use being made of the available space so that now there were six floors.

He climbed three flights of stairs, beginning to puff as he started on the third one. At the head was a small landing, on either side of which was a set of chambers. He turned left. The outer door was pinned back, displaying on its upper half a list of members; the names of those who were practising being in bold letters, while those who were merely associated with chambers were in light lettering. His name headed the list; occasionally, he spent a few seconds recalling the times when it had been at the bottom of the list of his first chambers. He opened the inner door and went in.

There was a passageway off which led five rooms, a cloakroom, and the clerks' room. A murmur of conversation came through the doorway of the clerks' room. He walked on, although normally he stopped to say good morning, a routine that started his working day.

He entered his room. Until he'd decided to apply for Silk, he'd always had a pupil who'd shared the room with him; since a Silk was not allowed to have a pupil, he'd not replaced the last one when that self-opinionated young man had reached the end of the year; now he had the room to himself—the only member of chambers to do so.

He hung his umbrella and hat on the mahogany stand, added his overcoat. He crossed to the desk and looked down at the several briefs, then walked past the shelves of books to the single large sash window. He stared out at the small square which consisted of grass and four small flowerbeds surrounded by a gravel path. Had the police found anything of significance? Was there anything they could find . . . ?

His thoughts were interrupted by a quick knock on the door. Arnold, the chief clerk, entered. He closed the door, carefully so that it made no noise, walked with his strange, almost mincing gait up to the desk, coughed once, and said: 'Good morning, sir.' His first greeting was always formal. After that, it would be 'Mr Elham'.

It struck Elham—with complete inconsequentiality— that he'd never before realized quite how ungainly Arnold was; as if head, arms, body, and legs, had not originally been meant for each other.

'Not a very nice morning. And the forecast is that the rain will become quite heavy.'

Elham returned to his desk, pulled out the chair, and slumped down on it. He was conscious that Arnold was looking at him with concern. 'I had a bit of a thick night, Tom.'

'Then there's no need to worry. You're not in court today.'
'I'm not?'

'I did mention it last thing last night. Wicks and Chamfers has been moved to Monday. Of course, that meant I had to do something about Stevens and Stevens, so I rang Mr Baldwin and explained and asked if it would be all right if

Mr Young took the brief. After a bit, he agreed.' Arnold sucked in his thick lower lip, then let it go with a plopping sound; a frequent mannerism of his when he was pleased with himself. 'I did suggest at the time that the brief wasn't really marked high enough.'

For once, Elham was uninterested in the markings on his briefs. Let the police gain even a hint that it might have been the Jaguar . . . But there'd been no eyewitnesses and now the original damage was completely masked . . .

'Are you all right, Mr Elham?'

Arnold, looking like a dehydrated dugong, was peering down at him with an expression of concern. 'Of course I'm all right,' he snapped.

'A very thick night!' Very occasionally, Arnold permitted himself a touch of familiarity; it was as out of character as a Stradivarius playing rock. Penelope often referred to him as Uriah Heep, but this nickname was inappropriate since however unctuous his manner, however ungainly his appearance, his sense of loyalty to Elham was unbounded.

The phone rang and Elham picked up the receiver. The caller said that he was passing on unofficial word that Elham's application to be granted Silk had been accepted. Congratulations and that was going to cost a couple of glasses of champagne at their next meeting.

Elham replaced the receiver and stared at the nearest brief on his desk. It was marked £500, of which Arnold would receive ten per cent. As a fashionable and successful Silk, briefs marked £5000 would be far from unusual. He said: 'I'll be taking Silk.'

'Congratulations, Mr Elham. Indeed, many, many congratulations. Not that I ever had the slightest doubt. It was merely a question of choosing the right time.' He was filled with excited pleasure and pride.

CHAPTER 4

The PC parked by the side of the road, stepped out and slammed the door shut. He looked at the oblong house and correctly judged that it had once been two primitive, semi-detached cottages which had been converted into one reasonably comfortable home. There were still two front doors, but no path across the lawn to either of them. He went along the cinder path to the back door. This was half glass and through it he could see a woman standing by a solid fuel cooker. He knocked and she walked across and opened the door. 'Mrs Daley?'

'That's right.' In contrast to his Kentish acent, she had a much harder, sharper London one.

'I'd be glad of a word with Mr Daley, if he's around.'

'He ain't. He's at work.'

'Where would that be?'

'At Mill Farm.'

'Which is where?'

She told him how to drive there, then her manner became slightly easier. 'I suppose it's on account of last night.'

'It is.'

'It real shook him.'

'It would.'

'Coming round the corner and seeing someone lying in the road . . . How is the poor man?'

'The last heard, he was still not conscious and they don't really know yet how badly injured he is.'

'And it was someone in a car what hit him and didn't stop?'

'That's right.'

'D'you know what I'd do to people like that?'

'No, missus, I don't, but I do know what I would
... Thanks a lot, then, sorry to have disturbed your
work.'

'I hopes you find the driver.'

'We will.'

He turned away and walked back to his car, hardly aware
of the distant view of farmland and woods. He'd been born
in the country, but was happy to live in a town. In winter,
the countryside was either knee deep in mud and muck or
frozen solid.

Mill Farm—there was no stream and no sign that there
had ever been a windmill—was on the right-hand side of
the road; a square, red brick house, uncompromisingly
functional, lay close to the road and leading past it was a
concrete drive which ended at a range of farm buildings
which dated from the same time as the house. Three wings
jutted out from the long, central building and the dairy was
in the near end of the middle one of these. Inside, a man
was cleaning down the sides of a large stainless steel bulk
milk tank. The emptying valve was open and the waste
water was gushing out on to the concrete floor; the PC had
to step carefully to avoid getting his shoes soaked. 'Mr
Daley?'

Daley nodded. A tall, thin man with a face tanned by sun
and wind, he spoke sparingly and moved with the slow,
regular action of someone who'd spent all his working life
with animals.

'I'd like a word if you've the time?'

He nodded again. He looped the hose over the side of the
tank so that the jet continued to play into it, went over to a
tap and turned this off. He moved across to a control panel,
opened a couple of valves and switched on a pump to
circulate cleaning fluid around the milk lines.

'D'you smoke?' asked the PC, producing a pack of cigarettes.

'Not in here I don't.'

The PC grinned. 'Sorry.'

'It's not me, it's the boss . . . D'you feel like a coffee?'

'I wouldn't say no to a cuppa.'

Daley led the way out of the dairy and round to the far wing and a small side room in which were a couple of wooden chairs, a butane gas-ring, and an old, deep stone sink above which was a tap. On the far side of the sink was a stained and battered table on which were a kettle, a jar of instant coffee, a jug of milk, a packet of sugar, a couple of teaspoons, and four earthenware mugs. He filled the kettle, lit the gas-ring, and put the kettle on this.

The PC sat, somewhat gingerly since the chair looked less stout than in fact it was, then said: 'It was you who found the injured man near the cricket field at Ailsham?'

'It were.'

'So maybe you can help us trace out the car which knocked him down?' He again brought out the pack of cigarettes from his pocket and this time Daley accepted one without demur. 'As I understand it, you came round the corner by the cricket field and there was the man in the road?'

'That's how it was.'

'And a bit before you reached the corner, you met a car going in the opposite direction?'

'Yes.' The kettle began to steam and Daley turned off the gas. 'How d'you like it—strong?'

'Not too strong, but then neither too weak. A bit like a Piccadilly whore.'

Daley did not smile. He spooned instant coffee into two of the mugs, lifted up the kettle, and poured in water. 'There's the milk and sugar. Ain't no call to worry how much milk you use.'

'You can always pump yourself up some more?' The PC stood, went over, helped himself to three spoonfuls of sugar and a generous measure of milk. He returned to his chair.

'This other car—d'you think the driver of that had seen the man in the road?'

'Can't think of no way he didn't.'

'How was the car being driven?'

'Fast.'

'What d'you mean by that?'

'What I says.'

The PC smiled. 'Would you like to give an estimate of its speed?'

'No, I wouldn't.'

'Was it going straight or weaving about a bit?'

Daley shrugged his shoulders. 'No saying. Never dipped his bloody lights so all I was worried about was seeing where I was going.'

'How many headlights did it have?'

'One.'

'One?'

'That's what I said, ain't it?'

'Which side was this?'

'Nearside.'

The preliminary findings were that the man had been hit by a car driving in the direction of Ailsham, well over on the wrong side of the road—the offside light would have taken the force of the blow. There had been a doctor who'd travelled with the ambulance and he'd judged that the accident had taken place within a short time—say a quarter of an hour—of his examination, so the accident had occurred very shortly before Daley had reached the scene. While the driver of this other car with only the nearside lights working might have been someone unwilling to become involved, it was, on present evidence, more reasonable to assume he was the hit-and-run driver. 'Can you suggest what kind of car it was?'

Daley spoke scornfully. 'I said, he never dipped. Blinded me, even if they was yellow.'

The PC didn't say that this was fresh evidence. The French always had yellow lights. If this had been a French car, the chances of identifying it became very slim unless the driver was caught at the port of embarkation with a smashed headlight and a dented wing (forensic evidence suggested the car must have suffered obvious, but not heavy, damage). 'You got no impression at all of what sort of car it was?'

Daley showed himself to be a stubborn man. 'Didn't you hear—I was blinded?'

'Sure. But even under those conditions one can still sometimes gain some sort of overall impression of a car. Have a go. Was it big or small?'

Daley drank, drew on his cigarette, then said, with some reluctance: 'Big.'

'What kind of big? Something like a Land-Rover?'

'No. It were one of them smooth jobs.'

It took a little time to determine that in this context smooth meant curved and sporty.

'A bit like a Ferrari, for instance?'

'What's that?'

'You must know what a Ferrari looks like.'

'Well, I bloody don't.'

Such ignorance was, in the eyes of a car enthusiast like the PC, quite heretical. There was something about having much to do with cows which addled a man's brains. He asked a few more questions, but it had become obvious that there was nothing more to be learned.

Rickmore crossed over to the window of his office and stared out. On the far side of the street, two boys were playing marbles under the bare branches of a large horse-chestnut tree. The course of their game eluded him since it bore no resemblance to any of the variations he had known in his youth. He turned, a shade too energetically, and winced.

The aspirins he'd taken after breakfast—a breakfast restricted to coffee—were having little effect and his head still thumped at about 9 on the Richter scale. It was damnably unfair that he should suffer so much since he hadn't been drunk, he'd merely drunk too much. When he'd complained to Anne, she'd shown a callous lack of sympathy. Alcohol always reacted badly on him, so why drink as much as he had?

He returned to his chair and carefully sat. He read what he'd written ten minutes earlier, scrumpled up the sheet of paper and threw it at the wastepaper basket. It dropped outside. It was just one of those mornings. He picked up his ballpoint pen, squared up a fresh sheet of paper, and thought. He thought that his headache was becoming worse and his stomach was revolting. The telephone rang and the assistant sales manager, overseas, asked him if he'd heard from Julot in Paris. He said he hadn't and as he replaced the telephone, he thought that that was hardly surprising. Selling refrigerators to Eskimos was a simple task compared to selling English perfumes to Parisians . . .

An old friend had said not long ago that all right, the job wasn't the best paid in the country, but who was he to complain when his life was spent in the company of glorious, glamorous, half-naked women? Impossible to make Mike understand that as PRO he was seldom, if ever, in the company of the frolicsome ladies who appeared in the firm's advertisements.

How to say something fresh about the firm's products? How to fill up the monthly newsletter with little snippets of information that would attract the attention of the press and so lead to a mention of those products in the newspapers? How to persuade the glossy magazines to add to their list of acknowledgements, perfumes by Teerson Products. Teerson Products sounded more like the manufacturers of pot scourers than seductive perfumes for exotic women. A suggestion he'd made soon after joining the firm had been that they change the name of the brand products to something more suited to the image they wanted to capture. The suggestion had been received with frosty disapproval. Mr Teerson was very, very proud of his name and wanted it heralded far and wide. A chemist by training, he'd discovered a way of making personable perfumes using wholly synthetic and cheap materials; the discovery had made him rich. Rich men paid poor men to glorify them, not to extinguish them under pseudonyms. Realizing that here was a verity which might repeatedly prevent him doing his job as effectively as he'd want to do it, he'd considered resigning and looking for a position where his ability would not be stifled by pride. But the recession had begun to bite hard and jobs had not been as easy to find as before and he simply hadn't been prepared to take the risk of finding himself unemployed for months on end . . . And to look on the cheerful side, the job was not demanding—one learned to overcome, or ignore, the frustration—and it did leave him time and energy for his writing . . .

He often wished he'd as much confidence in himself as an author as Anne had. Then he wouldn't ask himself if her confidence rested on loyalty rather than critical honesty. The public had received his one published book with a notable lack of acquisitive enthusiasm and his royalty returns had looked rather like a census of Jews living in Mecca —but his editor was always encouraging him and had stated with apparent honest authority that one day his books would become a critical and popular success . . . It was a strange fact that the only time Elham had treated him without the slightest condescension had been when he'd offered him one of the six free copies of his book. It did seem that somewhere within Elham's breast there lurked a faint respect for things other than financial success and social standings . . . He smiled. Since the book had, indirectly, questioned the integrity of success and the merit of wealth, Elham must have found the book very distasteful. Or perhaps he'd never bothered actually to read it. Certainly Penelope wouldn't have done. She never read anything but her horoscope and probably that occasionally taxed her intelligence . . .

He checked the time. Ten minutes to coffee. Two hours and ten minutes to lunch. Five hours and ten minutes to packing-up. And the end of another day devoted to furthering the future of Mr Teerson, private egotist, public philanthropist, and staunch defender of free enterprise's right to exploit its workers.

CHAPTER 5

Elham put the last of the accompanying documents down by the side of the twenty pages of instructions. At stake in this action was the contingent liability arising from alleged malfeasance under a contract in which the terms were ambiguous. Both sides had a case and one of the points of law at issue was highly arcane. Normally, it would have been just the kind of brief to please him. To begin with it was highly marked, and beyond that he was a born lawyer, enjoying the subtleties of shades of meaning and seeing nothing odd in spending endless time pondering the true significance of a single sentence. But today this case merely irritated him to the point where he wondered why the two parties couldn't summon up sufficient common sense to resolve their own difficulties. Today his mind repeatedly returned to that moment when the man had run out into the road, to be sent flying by the Jaguar . . . If only they'd left Oak Tree Cottage five minutes earlier or later. If only he'd driven a little slower or a little quicker . . .

How far had the police now got in their investigations?

Whatever happened, they couldn't possibly trace the car. Could they? There'd been no one else on the road, the victim could have seen nothing . . . Those whose work brought them close to the police knew that, often through no fault of their own, far from the highly successful crime detection force many believed them, they were frequently all at sixes and sevens. When there was no direct evidence of identity, it was probably true to say that they didn't solve four out of five hit-and-run cases. But that still left the one that was solved . . .

Years ago, soon after he'd been called, he'd defended a man from a good background who'd been accused of swindling the firm for whom he'd worked. During the course of one of the interviews, the man had said: 'I've discovered something. The worst thing is the fear, not the fact.' At the time, he'd not fully understood what the man had meant, but now he did.

He looked at the telephone. There must be someone he could speak to to discover what progress the police were making . . . Only a fool drew attention to himself by asking such questions . . . But he'd soon go bloody mad from the stress . . .

The question suddenly formed in his mind: Why didn't he see Lucy? However mentally tired he might be, she fed fresh life into him. Surely, then, she could also banish his fears? Never mind for once that it was the middle of the day. (He'd never been to her place during the day, only at night. Buried within his subconscious was the belief that daylight adultery was sordid.)

He collected his hat and overcoat and put these on, picked up his umbrella. He looked at the briefcase, but left it. He walked down the corridor to the clerks' room. Allwyn, one of the younger members of chambers, was talking to Betty Greer, Arnold's assistant. ''Morning T. E. I hear from the grapevine you're taking Silk. Congratulations.'

He muttered a few appropriate words.

'Don't forget, I never mind being led. Especially astray.'

Elham ignored that weak attempt at humour. He said to Betty: 'Where's Tom?'

Betty, fast approaching middle age, plumpish, level-headed, reliable and efficient, if slow, replied: 'He had to go across to the courts a moment ago; he'll be back soon.'

'When he does, tell him I've gone out and won't be returning until some time in the late afternoon.' He nodded at Allwyn, left. He wondered if Betty and Allwyn were now trying to guess what had caused him to act so out of character? If so, Allwyn would doubtless hint at something salacious, little realizing how right he was . . .

He walked along the road, past Middle Temple Hall, to Fleet Street. He stood on the edge of the pavement and hailed every approaching taxi; the fourth one was free and it stopped. 'Twenty-two, Cuthbertson Road,' he said, as he opened the back door.

'Is that at the back of Harrods, Guv?'

'That's right.' He settled on the back seat. In ten days' time, he thought, it would be a year since he'd first met Lucy at a cocktail party, given by acquaintances rather than friends, to which he'd not wanted to go, but had because Penelope had insisted they did. It was ironic that Penelope's insistence had been fuelled by the possibility that some rather important people would be present—they'd never turned up. There was even more, and harsher, irony in the fact that Penelope was so beautiful and desirable that at that party no man under the age of senility had looked at her without desire, yet she was totally uninterested in sex. At first, after their marriage, he'd put this down to shyness —even in a permissive age, perhaps not every woman permitted. But then, unwillingly, he'd been forced to understand that she just was not interested in the physical act of love because she gained no pleasure from it. She'd never actively rejected him. She didn't refuse his demands while inventing headaches, she simply never responded and nothing he had ever said or done had altered that fact. Finally accepting that that was the situation, he'd tried to come to terms with it logically. He gained physical pleasure from her body, so why should it matter to him that she gained none from his? The loss was hers, not his. But while the law might cherish logic, emotions did not. The more she denied him her passion, the more he longed for it, at the cost of his own pleasure . . .

At the cocktail party—composed, as he'd previously guessed, of people right outside his milieu and of little consequence to him—he'd been cornered by a man who had been castigating the latest negotiating platform of the printing unions with boring fluency when Lucy had come up and said that his wife wasn't feeling too well and she wanted to go home. 'Not again, for God's sake!' the man had exclaimed bitterly. After he'd left, Lucy had said: 'I do so hate that kind of comment. It leaves one vainly wondering whether she's tight, pregnant, or just a hypochondriac.'

'Don't you know?' he'd said, surprised that he responded to her uncalled-for comments instead of ignoring them.

'How on earth could I when I've only just met the woman?'

'Then wouldn't it have been better . . .' He stopped, realizing—just in time—that now it was he who was in danger of ignoring a basic rule of social conversation.

She'd grinned, a mischievous, challenging grin. 'Wouldn't it have been better if I'd minded my own business? Of course. But then think how much more boring . . . Are you Lloyd's, lawyer, or layabout in the Foreign Office?'

'Why should I be any of those?'

'The mould's unmistakable.'

'I've no idea what you mean.'

'Then there's no point in my explaining, because you'd never understand.'

That night, as he and Penelope had prepared for bed— separate beds—she'd said: 'Who was that extraordinary women you were talking to for such a long time? The one dressed so outrageously in stretch pants.'

For some reason, which he'd not then attempted to analyse, he'd answered with defensive brevity. 'God only knows! I was stuck with her when she came across with a message for someone I'd been talking to before.'

'Oh!' Penelope had ceased to be interested in the woman whose social tastes were so obviously lacking.

Lucy had haunted his mind. She'd appear without warning when he was shaving, when Penelope asked him what he thought of her new frock, when he started to read the law reports in the train, when Arnold spoke about the latest brief to come in to chambers. Since he tried to hide himself from himself as well as from other people, it had been quite some time before he'd accepted the fact that she was haunting his mind because he was convinced, even on so short an acquaintance, that in her the fires of passion didn't just burn, they raged. Once this acceptance was made, her images became lascivious.

He'd managed to hold the haunting images in check for a time, then they had become too febrile to be contained any longer. One Thursday he'd set out to identify the small, sparkling, outrageous woman whose eyes had suggested, whose mouth had demanded, whose body had promised. He'd telephoned the host of the party, spent several minutes discussing matters of no consequence, then had casually introduced the one that had come to concern him so deeply.

'You mean it was Lucy you were talking to?'

'That's right.'

'I wish I'd known that. I'd have listened in.'

'Why?' he'd asked, with pompous stiffness.

'Because I can't imagine a more disparate duo and it would have been amusing to hear you misunderstanding each other. Did she shatter your remaining faith in femininity?'

'As a matter of fact, I did find her rather forthright.'

'What you mean is, plain bloody rude. Her trouble is, she's fruity.'

For some reason, impossible to recall, he had accepted this as a slang word, not met before, for lesbians. He'd known a sharp, and clearly illogical, sense of loss. 'Is she? I must say, she didn't strike me as one, but you just can't tell these days, can you?'

'She didn't strike you as one what?'

'Lesbian.'

'Lucy? She'd die of laughing if you told her that. What ever gave you such a crazy idea?'

'You said she was fruity.'

Another bellow of laughter. 'I've always said that you lawyers know less about the world you live in than a newborn babe . . . As fruity as a nut cake. Nutty. As mad as they come.'

'She's rather unusual?'

'My God, you've only got to see some of her sculptures to know that. Why d'you think one of the Sunday papers keeps referring to her as an up-and-coming sculptress?' An even louder bellow of laughter, the reason for which Elham only discovered later. 'So why all the interest? Thinking of joining her lists?'

'Good God, no!'

'It makes a lovely thought. From what I hear, in five minutes flat—' a pause, for that to be appreciated—'she'd have a misogynist renouncing his faith.'

For a time, he'd struggled with himself. He was a sober, decent, respectable husband; sober, decent, respectable husbands did not betray their marriages, even in modern times . . . It was, of course, true that Penelope refused him her passion—but many men were refused not only passion but body as well, and yet they continued to honour their marriages . . .

Now that it had been confirmed that by repute she was every bit as passionate as he'd imagined, the mental images became too painful to be borne. He'd telephoned her on the Friday. 'My name is Terence Elham. I don't suppose you'll remember me . . .'

'Then you lack supposition. Ever since that ghastly cocktail party, I've been wondering if you really can be as starchy as you appear.'

He'd taken a taxi to her flat and as he'd climbed out on to the pavement, he'd become aware of the fact that he was clammy from sweat. He'd almost returned into the taxi . . .

She'd been wearing a loose pair of overalls and—it seemed to him—little else, since the day was warm. The gently outlined flesh beneath the overalls, changing shape as she moved, had excited him to the point where his breath became short . . .

She'd led the way through to her studio because, she'd said, she'd a spot of work to finish before she showered and changed and they went out to dinner. She'd suggested they had a drink right away and had asked him to pour her a Campari and whatever he wanted for himself. Several bottles and half a dozen glasses had been on a tray on a table against the far wall. Next to that table had been a second and much larger one and on this had been a few of her sculptures. He'd examined them with an interest which initially turned to puzzlement, then to consternation, when he realized he was looking at the male member, in virile state, cast in the form of Cleopatra's Needle, the Eiffel Tower, the Post Office Tower, Nelson's Column, the Empire State Building, and the Leaning Tower of Pisa.

'Wonderful!'

Slack-jawed, he'd turned and stared at her.

'I bet myself you'd react exactly as you have. I am going to enjoy getting to know you very, very much.'

For dinner, she'd chosen a nearby restaurant, dimly-lit and smoochy, on the grounds that it would be as different as possible from the places to which he normally went. It was. Afterwards they'd walked to her flat arm-in-arm—something he hadn't done in years—and the smile on her face had been tantalizing, promising, and triumphant . . .

The taxi came to a stop. He climbed out and paid, adding an exact tip. He went up the stone stairs to the front doorway, recessed under a portico, and pressed the top button on the answerport. Lucy's voice came through the speaker loud and clear.

'I've got to see you.'

'Terry?' From the first day, she'd used the diminutive because he'd told her that no one else did. 'What the hell's up?'

'I . . . I need you.'

There was a buzz as the door catch was released. He went inside and climbed the stairs to the third floor. She was standing in the doorway and he saw she was wearing the same overalls as she had on his first visit. She stared at him, her expression intense. 'You really do need me?'

'Yes,' he said hoarsely.

She put her arms round him and pressed him to herself. 'Shall I tell you something, my lovely lawyer? Those are the sweetest words you could say to me.'

CHAPTER 6

Ridley left his office and went along the passage to the lift, found it was up at the top floor, and decided to go down the stairs. These brought him to the outside door on the north side of the building. The wind had become stronger and colder and it made him wish he'd had the sense to bring his mackintosh; for a moment he thought about returning to get it, but decided it wasn't worth the bother.

He walked briskly up Bank Street, turned left into High Street and the pedestrian precinct, and continued along this to the laundry. The redhead behind the counter greeted him with a smile. ''Afternoon. Getting chilly, isn't it? Bart says he thinks we're in for snow.'

'Tell him from me that he's a miserable old b.'

'Don't you like snow?'

'Well, do you?'

'If there's enough of it. Then the roads get blocked and I can't come in to work.'

'It's all right for some! If I had a six-foot drift all round my house, the boss would just expect me to grab a shovel and start digging . . . Have you got my jacket?'

'Where's the ticket?'

'Sorry and all that, love, but I forgot to bring it from home.'

'Then you're out of luck.'

'Sports jacket, a kind of a check in green and grey, with black stripes in all directions.'

'Suppose I tell you we've fifty jackets like that?'

'I wouldn't believe you.'

'Men!'

'Where would you be without 'em?'

'Happier.' She sighed. 'All right, I'll see what I can do.'

'That's my girl.'

'Yeah. Just so long as I do what you want.'

'Is that an offer?'

'Didn't you once tell me you was married?'

'She's generous.'

'I'm not.' She left and went through swing doors, careful to move her hips with grace.

He remained by the counter and stared out through the glass door. Still nothing on the hit-and-run victim, despite reference to the local and national missing persons' lists . . . Odd that so far no one had come forward to report a husband, son, or lodger missing. The man had been in good physical shape, so he hadn't been living rough—someone must know he hadn't returned to his home, even if that someone was only an inquisitive neighbour. Another odd thing, there'd been no means of identification on him; most people carried around with them personal papers of one sort or another. And where had he been going at that time of night on foot (there'd been no parked car nearby) . . .

The redhead pushed open one of the swing doors and returned into the shop, in her right hand a flimsy wire hanger on which hung a sports jacket. 'This is the only one like you described.'

'Thought you'd got fifty? That's mine, all right; straight from Savile Row. You're a marvellous girl.'

'I know.' Expertly, she extracted the hanger, folded the coat, and wrapped it in brown paper. 'That's four quid.'

'Christ! Started cleaning 'em in champagne?' He paid her and left.

Lucy gently ran the tips of her fingers down Elham's chest. 'Now tell me what the matter is.'

'Nothing.'

'Don't be silly. When you said you needed me, I thought you were just extra horny. But you needed to screw me because you're in some sort of trouble and it's a way of getting some relief.'

He hated it when she spoke so crudely.

'Come on, tell me what's biting you—apart from me . . . Nothing's ever so bad as it seems when you keep it to yourself.' She leaned over and gently nibbled his right breast.

'Last night . . .' He stopped.

'What about it?'

'We went to dinner with my brother-in-law.'

'I don't suppose that was enough to knock you sideways, so what went wrong there?'

'I was driving back afterwards and . . . and there was an accident.'

'Your wife was hurt?'

'It wasn't like that, it was . . .' He stopped once more, then spoke quickly. 'I was driving very slowly and carefully, I swear I was. But suddenly this man ran out from some trees, straight in front of the car. There wasn't anything I could do. You've got to understand, there wasn't anything at all I could do because there wasn't the time. It all happened too quickly.'

'You hit him?'

'Only a little,' he answered, quite unaware of the absurdity of his words.

'Was he badly hurt?'

'Not really.'

'Surely no one can begin to blame you, if you didn't even have time to brake?'

'I swear I didn't.'

'Love, you mustn't torture yourself like this, if there was nothing you could do.'

'There wasn't.'

'Well, then . . . Sometimes things happen which there's just no way of avoiding. And if this man wasn't seriously hurt, you've no need to go on worrying about him.' She kissed him, full-mouthed, hungrily. 'Are you going to remember that now?'

He wanted to tell her the full story so that she could agree he'd done the only sensible thing and that it would have been absurd for him to risk the destruction of his career, but he couldn't be certain that he'd still hold her sympathy; she had some odd ideas . . .

She nibbled his ear. 'Are you going to remember that now?'

'Yes.'

'Then maybe you'll screw me because you want to, not to help you forget last night?'

Emmery was twenty and ambitious. And he possessed the instinct which told him a story was stronger than the facts so far in evidence suggested which was the hallmark of a good journalist.

He said, over the phone: 'Then you've still no idea who he is?'

'That's right.'

'He doesn't fit anyone on the missing list?'

'No.'

He asked a few more questions, to which he received unsatisfactory answers, rang off. He didn't think the police were deliberately playing it close to their chests—they really had no idea who the injured man was. But who, other than a drop-out, could go missing without someone trying to trace him?

He told the news editor that he'd a lead which looked promising, OK to follow it up? The editor agreed. Emmery left the square, dirt-stained building, crossed to the much-used Nova, climbed in, started the engine, and drove out on to the road.

It was an eighteen-mile drive to Reckton, through gently rolling, well farmed countryside with the North Downs as a backdrop. At the large roundabout immediately outside the town, he took the second exit.

Thirty years before, Reckton had been a market town, unremarkable, but possessing a quiet, rather sleepy charm. Then the railway line to London had been electrified, bringing the town within the commuter belt, and the planners had been let loose, their brief to modernize and enlarge in order to cope with the projected increase in population. With unerring instinct, they'd destroyed all that was worth preserving and preserved all that should have been destroyed. Now, the town was without a soul.

They'd changed the course of the ring road since he'd last used it and he missed the turning he wanted. He found there was no right turn at the next junction so had to take the one after that and, swearing freely, finished up in an area he did not know. Inevitably, the first person he asked for directions was a stranger, but the second was not and she directed him to the hospital.

He spoke to a sister who answered his questions as briefly and generally as possible. The patient was still in a coma, in intensive care. He had suffered chest and arm injuries, but these were relatively minor; far more serious had been the blow to his skull which had fractured it and caused internal bleeding and possibly further injury, the extent of which could not yet be determined. It was impossible to give any sort of prognosis. No one had visited him.

Emmery returned to the Nova. It was odd, he thought, to be lying in hospital, in a coma, unidentified—it made of him a no-man. Which suggested the heading, The Abominable No-man . . .

He drummed on the wheel with his fingers. He'd discovered nothing solid that would build a story. At best, unknown man lying in a coma after hit-and-run accident might make for a small filler in next Tuesday's *Gazette*. But, now that he was here, it seemed a pity to return to Etchinstone without following up his hunch a bit further . . . Surely it was worth questioning the man who'd discovered the victim?

Daley was milking. Five at a time, the Friesians came into alternate sides of the herringbone milking parlour where they were fed automatically while he clamped on the clusters.

'I wonder if you've time for a word?' shouted Emmery, as he stood on the steps leading down to the pit.

Daley looked briefly up at him. 'Does it look like I've nothing to do?' He removed the cluster from the end cow on the right-hand side, glanced along the row of bags (which, from the pit, was almost all he could see of the cows), pulled down on a lever which opened a gate and allowed the cows to make their way out of the standings and the parlour. He closed that gate, opened the far one, pulled on a rope which slid back the door into the collecting yard. Cows came through and he shut the door behind the fifth one, then the gate. He sponged down the bags. A cow urinated and the hot liquid splashed down on the concrete and rebounded. Emmery hurriedly retreated and Daley showed his sarcastic amusement.

'I'm from the *Gazette*,' Emmery said, once satisfied he was safe.

Daley dropped the cloth back into the bucket of disinfectant. It took all sorts to make a world.

'You found the injured man after the accident, didn't you?'

He picked up the first of the clusters from its hook, arranged the cups over his hand in a star pattern with the rubber tubes twisted to block the vacuum, placed the cluster under the first cow's bag, in turn untwisted each cup and slipped it over a teat.

'It was you who found the injured man, wasn't it?'

He nodded.

'It must have been a bit of a shock?'

He moved down to the second cow.

'And you also saw the car that hit him?'

'I saw a car; that's all.'

'But the police think . . .'

'What they think is their business; it ain't mine.'

Emmery smiled; he rather liked awkward characters.

'They say that you said one of the car's headlights wasn't working, so since the man could only just have been knocked over, it like as not was that car. What make was it?'

'How would I know?'

'I thought you told the police?'

'Then you thought wrong.'

'What did you actually tell 'em, then?'

'Same as I'll tell you now, before you clear out of here and leave me to do me work. It was a big, smooth car and it was going fast.'

'You can't make a guess at what kind it was?'

'No. And the police can say it were a Ferrari from now until Christmas and it won't make no bloody difference.'

'Then it probably was a Ferrari?'

'I said I don't know.'

Emmery left, glad to escape the dangers of urinating cows. He walked through the dairy to his car. A Ferrari was a rich man's car . . . Unknown victim seriously injured by wealthy hit-and-run driver . . . That could make a story. And if it was angled adroitly, one or more of the London papers might pick it up, with financial advantage to himself.

They were watching a nature programme on BBC1 when the telephone rang. 'I'll get it,' Rickmore said. Anne loved films about birds, but he'd seen so many recently that they were beginning to bore him. He went out into the hall and crossed to the corner cupboard on which the telephone stood.

Penelope said: 'Dennis, I just had to ring and say how very much we both enjoyed last night. It was such fun to be with just the two of you.'

Was that an oblique way of saying that a dinner-party should always be composed of at least two couples other than the hosts? 'It was fun seeing you,' he replied.

'Anne's a wonderful cook; that mousse was simply the nicest I've ever eaten. You're a very lucky man.'

'And perhaps she's a lucky woman?'

'As I've always said, you're the perfect husband.'

Even Penelope ought to have choked on that piece of hypocrisy, he thought. 'Sounds to me as if we'd start favourites for the Dunmow flitch.'

'I'm sure you would.'

He was convinced she hadn't understood the reference. It occurred to him that she sounded even falser and more brittle than usual. 'How's Terence?'

'He's all right. Why shouldn't he be?'

'No reason, except I thought maybe he's still suffering from the remains of a hangover.'

'Don't be ridiculous. He had nothing of the sort.'

Even if he had been slightly tactless in his words, it seemed odd that she should have responded so sharply. He tried to pour a little verbal oil. 'If he was lucky, I wasn't. I spent most of the morning wondering whether to cut my throat to end the agony.'

'Terence did not have too much to drink last night.'

'Lucky man.'

'He was perfectly sober when we left you.'

'Couldn't have been more so.' He managed to keep the irony from his voice.

There was a brief pause. 'Will you tell Anne how much we enjoyed ourselves?'

'I will.'

'Goodbye.'

He'd never before known her to end a telephone conversation so abruptly. Usually, there were protestations of regret at having to ring off and promises to meet again just as soon as the so-crowded social calendar permitted . . .

He returned to the sitting-room. The nature film was finished and the credits were showing.

'Turn off, sweet,' she said.

'Let's just see what's on next . . .'

'It's that awful series where people get beaten up every five minutes. I can't stand so much violence.'

He switched off the television set.

'Who was that on the phone?'

'Your sister, making her bread-and-butter call.'

'How is she?'

'Same as ever, except not quite.'

'A very intelligent answer!'

He went over and rumpled her hair and she grabbed his hand and dragged it down, then pressed it once in a silent message of love before releasing it. 'What's wrong with Penny?'

'Nothing definite, but her manner was a bit odd.'

'I thought that as far as you're concerned, it always is?'

'Maybe I should have said, odder than usual. When I asked her how his lordship was because he might have had a touch too much vino last night, she took considerable um.'

'For goodness sake, what d'you expect? You really are quite hopeless.'

'If she'd said that about me to you, would you have become really huffy?'

'Of course not, but I'm not Penny.'

'For which the gods be thanked.' He crossed to his chair. 'Come to think of it, they were both a bit odd when I returned his glasses last night.'

'If you want my opinion, in the state you were in everyone and everything was odd. I should never have let you drive. There could so easily have been another terrible accident.'

He stared at the wood fire, flames dancing high. 'Have you heard any more about that?'

'No, but then I've only been to the local shops.'

'Usually, that's the source of all news.'

'Gossip, not news.'

He yawned. 'How about making tracks for bed? . . . Rejoice! Tomorrow's Friday, the last working day of the week.'

'Do you really hate the job all that much?'

'I suppose not. After all, it's no more unnecessary and vapid than most and as far as I know the firm's products haven't ever actually killed anyone.'

'But you wish you were at home, writing?'

'That's the masochistic streak in me.'

'Don't be so stupid, and stop denigrating your own work. One day, you'll be famous.'

'But for what?'

CHAPTER 7

The laboratory assistant stared at the ancient Olympia typewriter with dislike. His training assured him that it was ridiculous to credit a piece of machinery with a diabolical sense of humour, but this machine had one. Why else should it type Y every time he meant to strike T?

He pulled out the form from the roller, scrumpled it up, and threw it into the wastepaper basket. He threaded in a fresh form and started typing once more. Reference number, source of exhibit, remitting police officer, date of receipt, date of examination, name of examiner . . . So far, only one typing error and that easily covered up since an n could be turned into a reasonable h. He resumed typing. Description of exhibit, results of examinations . . . One very small sliver of glass recovered from sweater, sample too small for comparison tests but consistent with glass from a vehicle's headlamp; quantity of dirt, pulverized and forced into jeans,

probably by impact, containing traces of brick dust and very
fine sawdust—type of wood . . .

He reached the end of the report, gratified by the fact
that in all he'd made only three unimportant errors. He
signed with a flourish, then noted that the time recorded
was 110P hours. He swore, as he changed the P into a 0
with a pen. That bloody typewriter!

The Detective-Inspector was a man who suffered constant
frustration because he tried to have almost every case which
came in fully investigated, even though he knew that there
was neither the manpower nor the time available to do this.
The trouble was, MacMahon had joined the CID in an era
of much less lawlessness when it had been possible to deal
efficiently with all but the very minor crimes and he'd never
been able to come to terms with a time when even a burglary
might be left to a uniform PC.

He scratched the top of his head, then tried to smooth the
remaining hair to hide his baldness. 'How's the Pierce job
going?'

Ridley answered: 'John's got that in hand, but so far he's
not had any breaks.' Had he ever been asked, he'd have
said that the DI was soft to work himself so hard; there were
no medals for growing ulcers. Not that Ridley viewed his
work with a cynical detachment. But he did divide it into
crime against property and against the person; the one was
a fact of life, the other an obscenity. No one could work
harder than he in a case involving the mugging of an old
woman or the raping of a young one, and had he had his
way those guilty would have been punished with physical
violence so that they could taste the pain, the terror, the
humiliation, of what they had inflicted.

'John?' The DI looked up. 'Doesn't the case call for
someone a bit sharper?'

'Maybe. But do we pull that someone off something else?'

One of the two telephones rang and the DI picked up the receiver. He listened, muttered a few words, replaced the receiver. 'The victim of the hit-and-run at Ailsham—he's just died without ever regaining consciousness.'

'Poor sod!'

'Not heard from Dabs yet?'

'Not a word. But we'll be near the bottom of their priority list on that job.'

'And there are no other leads as to the man's identity?'

'None.'

'It's strange he's not been reported missing.' MacMahon fiddled with a pencil. 'And nothing leading to the car?'

'You've got my report mentioning the yellow headlights? And the one which arrived from the lab this morning?'

The DI indicated the uneven pile of papers in front of himself. 'None of that takes us very far.'

'Doesn't take us any bloody where.' Ridley's tone was hard. The driver of the car hadn't given a damn about his victim; all he'd been interested in was saving his own skin. The car could well have been large and expensive, in which case the driver was a wealthy man. If there was one type of person Ridley scorned more than a coward, it was a rich coward.

Lucy's father had been a creative potter of a somewhat anarchical turn of mind and before her marriage her mother, daughter of a shopkeeper, had happily worked in a bank. It was, so Lucy claimed, this dichotomy of parental characteristics which left her a walking encyclopædia of contradictions.

She believed she was entitled to say and do whatever she wanted; but there were some things that she would never say and some she would never do. She believed that social conventions were ridiculous and so deliberately flouted them; but there were one or two she always observed and there was no logic in the distinctions. She went out of her way to shock; but would never shock if to do so might cause hurt. She was a pacifist and very CND, but she was extremely patriotic. She despised wealth, but liked the things that money bought. She demanded that each person be independent, yet allowed no exception to the rule that every individual on earth owed a love and a duty to every other.

She started breakfast at half past one, not because it was now everybody else's lunch-time, but because she had enjoyed a couple of joints the previous night and they always made her sleep like the dead. The simile bothered her. What was death? Would she know she was dead? If so, part of her mind must have lived on and therefore she could not be dead; if not, how could death have any meaning to the person it most concerned? . . . Such thoughts troubled her deeply and depressed her and it was then that she created her priapic sculptures. After all, one couldn't get any further away from death than the start of life. And ever since that first *succès de scandale* such sculptures had sold well, which meant she could spend and spend and prove to herself that she was alive . . .

She buttered a piece of toast, cut a large section of Edam and put this on the toast, reached across the debris-laden table for the jar of Hero black cherry jam. She claimed it was her Welsh ancestors who gave her her liking for jam with cheese. As far as she knew, she didn't have any Welsh ancestors.

As she ate, she skimmed through the *Guardian*. As a person of unimpeachable liberal outlook, she would have countenanced no other daily paper. On Sunday, however, she had the *Sunday Telegraph*. On Sundays, she was a reactionary.

Wars, threats of wars, politicians behaving like children, children behaving like politicians . . . And a brief report on a road accident near the village of Ailsham on Wednesday night in which an as yet unidentified man had been knocked down and seriously injured by a hit-and-run driver. Nothing was spelled out, yet everything was there for those who could read between the lines. The driver was wealthy, the victim was poor. The driver had been drunk, the victim hadn't had a chance. The driver had fled, careless of the fact that medical attention might be essential to save the victim's life . . .

Elham had told her that he'd been in an accident on Wednesday night, near Ailsham. But he'd said he'd been driving very carefully, it had not been his fault, and the man had not been seriously injured; his silence had implied that he'd naturally stopped and done what he could to help. All lies. He'd been drunk, the accident had been wholly his fault, and he'd abandoned the severely injured victim without a second's thought. He'd lied to gain her sympathy and she'd given it, whereas had she known the truth . . . A woman of sharp, occasionally overpowering emotions, she knew the anger and contempt which swept away all rational thought. Without giving herself time to consider her actions, she went across to the desk, picked up the telephone receiver, dialled 999, and when the operator asked her which emergency service she wanted, replied 'Police' in a tone which turned the word into one of moral violence.

CHAPTER 8

MacMahon drove into the courtyard at the back of the concrete and glass divisional HQ and parked in a free space. Before climbing out of the car, he raised the collar of his overcoat to try to ward off the north wind which had started blowing. He saw Ridley approach, obviously wanting to speak to him, and he gloomily decided that this meant more trouble.

'I'm glad I've caught you, sir.'

MacMahon was intrigued by that 'sir'. Most of the youngsters eschewed such a form of respect these days; instead, being television fans, they called him 'guv'nor'. But at their first meeting of the day, Ridley usually called him 'sir'. He would have liked to know why. He doubted it was a sign of respect. 'Don't tell me what the trouble is, let me guess. The mayor's been shot, the chairman of the county council has been found chasing little girls, and the police committee has named me fascist pig.'

Ridley didn't smile. 'We've had a call from London to tell us that a woman, who refused to identify herself, has been in touch to say that if the police want to know who was driving the hit-and-run car at Ailsham, they need to talk to Terence Elham.'

MacMahon walked towards the building, hurrying because the wind was giving his balding head a bad time. 'Elham . . . The name rings a bell, but for the moment, I'm damned if I can remember why.'

'I've asked around. He's a fairly prominent barrister.'

'Hell!' said MacMahon, just before he opened the door to go inside. The building was well heated and as they came to a stop by the lift, he lowered the collar of his coat. 'My old sergeant used to say that if you had the chance to choose between the Devil and a lawyer, settle for the Devil every time . . . What more d'you know?' He pressed the call button.

'Apart from the fact that he lives in Ailsham, nothing.'

The lift arrived and they took it to the fifth floor, walked along the corridor to the DI's room. MacMahon hung up his overcoat, then went round the desk and sat. 'Tim might be able to fill the picture in a bit.' He looked up a number, dialled it, spoke briefly. He thanked the other, replaced the receiver. 'Elham's a prominent junior barrister who's expected to take Silk very soon. A good all-rounder, hot on contract, well known at the criminal bar. He's rated as tough and clever and never hesitates to knock the police when he's defending.'

'One of them! Then it'll be a positive pleasure to land him.'

MacMahon leaned back in his chair. 'Maybe. But just remember that when you're dealing with a man with his background, if you've got any sense you'll go carefully.'

Typical! thought Ridley, with sudden anger. Just because the man didn't come from the slums, he had to be treated with kid gloves. Hadn't the DI realized the world had moved on? If it was Elham who'd knocked the man down and had then run, he deserved . . .

'His kind defend themselves with very heavy guns,' said MacMahon quietly. 'I'm trying to protect you, not him.' He saw that he was not believed. He sighed. Some people never learned, except the hard way. He hated violence and the waves of suffering it generated, just as much as Ridley, but he had learned long ago that meeting it with any kind of further violence was seldom satisfactory. He looked at his watch. 'The odds are, Elham's up in London. Tomorrow's Saturday, so he'll be at home all day.'

'I'll drive there . . .'

'We'll drive there,' MacMahon corrected.

Saturday was overcast. The clouds were dirt-coloured and they threatened rain or sleet; the increasing north wind suggested that sleet was the more likely.

In the room he used as a study—it had originally been the housekeeper's bedroom—Elham looked through the window and saw Juana, shopping basket in her left hand, come through the gateway into the drive and walk towards the back door, passing out of sight as she drew abreast of the small greenhouse. They'd been fortunate to find the Carvajals, he thought, with the complacency of someone who believed he was entitled to good fortune. Juana was an excellent cook and Miguel a reasonable gardener and neither believed in wasting time. Originally, he remembered, he'd been slightly reluctant to employ them because they might have left Chile for political reasons and he'd had no desire to support a couple of reds, but at no time since then had either of them ever shown the slightest sign of political awareness. And perhaps, his thoughts continued, considering how difficult it had become to find any servants, let alone good ones, a few left-wing sympathies—as opposed to activity—were not all that important.

He looked away from the window and down at the nearest brief on his desk. It was from Marsden & Slingfolds. Craig, the senior partner, had asked Arnold whether Mr Elham was thinking of taking Silk. Arnold's reply had been evasive and thus, in effect, an answer. Craig had then said good, there'd be quite a bit of work for Mr Elham, QC . . . To take or not to take Silk was a question which usually caused much heartburning. That one was a busy junior was no guarantee that one would become a busy Silk, since the junior was the all-rounder, the Silk the specialist. Further, Silks, to all intents and purposes, never appeared in court on their own, but always had juniors. This meant two sets of fees, with the Silk's noticeably higher than the junior's. So Silks were only briefed in major cases or where the client was wealthy, and therefore the amount of work potentially available was far less than when they'd been juniors; successful Silks made far more money than successful juniors, unsuccessful ones, far less. Many had discovered the bitter truth of this, but always too late. That ambition dug its own pit became very clear when one saw an underemployed Silk earning far less than he had, yet prevented from reverting to being a junior . . .

His thoughts changed course. It wasn't too fanciful to compare himself now with a man who'd awoken from a terrifying nightmare thankfully to find himself surrounded by the familiar, safe world. There'd been a short article in one of the papers about the hit-and-run case and this had named the car as a Ferrari. If that was what the authorities believed, then he could stop worrying . . .

He heard the front doorbell chime. Stephanie? Penelope said she might be calling. If so, he'd stay right where he was. Stephanie was loud-voiced; she was horsey and, like so many horsey people, had the manners of a groom; she was often downright rude to him. If she had not been so closely connected with one of the county families, Penelope and he would have had nothing to do with her.

He heard footsteps approach just before Penelope came into the room. 'Terence, two detectives have called and want to have a word with you.'

The icy waves of shock swept over him.

She closed the door and came up to the desk. 'For heaven's sake, pull yourself together.'

'But . . . but . . .'

'They'll be questioning everyone. But if they see you as you're looking right now, they won't need to question anyone else.'

'Why have they come here?'

'Why not? It's the biggest house in the village. They're bound to start with us.'

Were they?

'Just answer their questions. Don't volunteer anything.'

With a sense of bitter irony, he identified that as the advice he had given to many of his clients.

'And act as if you've absolutely nothing to worry about.'

He was again surprised to discover how sharp and cool she was, qualities with which, before the accident, he would never have credited her. In the face of such determination,

he forced himself to subdue and overcome his fears . . .
They could ask all the questions they liked, but he'd taken
steps to make certain that no one could ever prove the
truth . . .

Both men came to their feet as he entered the sitting-room.
MacMahon was dressed in an old, badly cut, heavily creased
suit; he had a round face, pleasantly featured, which looked
drawn, as if from long-term fatigue. A typically hardwork-
ing, but not over-intelligent middle-aged detective-
inspector. The detective-sergeant was much younger and
clearly far less tolerant and far more self-opinionated. Elham
spoke carefully, not hurrying his words; he was satisfied that
he sounded confident. 'I understand from my wife that you'd
like a word with me? Do sit down. And may we offer you
something to drink? Or, if it's too early, some coffee?'

'That's very kind of you,' replied MacMahon, as he sat,
'but we had a cup before we left.'

Elham walked over to the fireplace, turned to face the
room, and joined his hands together behind his back. By
taking that pose, he was reminding them that he was the
master of the house, successful, and wealthy. 'I'm a busy
man, so perhaps you'd tell me quickly how I can help?'

'That's easily answered, Mr Elham. We're looking for
someone who can tell us something about that hit-and-run
on Wednesday night . . . I don't know whether you've
heard, but the victim has unfortunately died.'

'Has he?' He was very conscious of the fact that his tone
had changed.

'So we are dealing with a very serious case. Is there any
way you can help us in identifying the driver of the car
concerned?'

Penelope was looking at him with an expression he had
no difficulty in reading. The death of the man altered
nothing; keep calm. 'No, I'm afraid I can't. If I had been
able to, I'd have been in touch with you before now.'

'Yes, of course.' MacMahon spoke so easily as to sound almost deferential. 'And you haven't heard any rumours?'

'I do not listen to rumours.'

'You don't? I suppose that's fair enough. Although just once in a while we find that a rumour does have some truth in it.'

'Really?'

MacMahon smiled. 'You remain unconvinced.'

'I do. And I am quite unable to suggest who might have been driving the Ferrari.'

'Ferrari?'

'That is the make of car the paper mentioned.'

'Oh, that! A typical load of cod's. Right now, we've no idea what make it was, except that it was a sporty model.'

'What does that mean?'

'Some kind of sports saloon; or maybe even an exotic.'

'Then it might have been a Ferrari?'

'Indeed. But, as I said, we've nothing as yet to suggest a make . . . That seems to be that, then.'

Ridley, sounding annoyed, said: 'What about—'

MacMahon interrupted. 'But I suppose we'd better just ask you the same question we're asking everyone else. Where were you on Wednesday night?'

'Has that any relevancy?'

'Only to this extent, that if you were out and returned here roughly about the time of the accident, you might have seen something that could help us. Were you out that night?'

'Yes.'

'Do you mind saying where?'

'We dined with my sister-in-law and her husband.'

'Where do they live?'

'Yew Cross.'

'So they're almost in the next village . . . It's like my brother-in-law. And, frankly, I never know whether that's a good thing or a bad one.' He smiled briefly. 'Have you any idea what the time was when you got back here?'

'No, not really.'

'We left there just after ten-thirty,' said Penelope firmly.

'Which road would you have returned on?'

'The usual one.'

'I'm sorry, Mrs Elham, but I'm afraid I don't know which is your usual road,' MacMahon said good-humouredly.

'Three Oaks crossroads and then direct to here.'

'Would that take you past the cricket field?'

'Yes.'

'About what time d'you think you'd have passed there?'

She shrugged her shoulders. 'Sometime between twenty and a quarter to.'

'In other words, a little before the accident. Did you by any chance see anyone walking along the road near the cricket ground?'

Elham answered. 'There were no pedestrians.'

'Did you observe any car which, in the broadest sense, could be termed sporty?'

'We met only one car that I can remember, at the cross-roads, it was an ordinary saloon.'

'Then now that finally is everything and we don't have to bother you any longer.' MacMahon stood. 'Thanks very much for your help.'

'I've hardly been able to help,' said Elham, a shade more forcefully than he'd intended.

'Maybe not directly, but indirectly, yes. We now know for certain that just before a quarter to eleven there was no sign of the victim walking along the road, or of a sporty car . . . Which does jog my memory. Just for the records, what kind of car do you run?'

'A Jaguar and my wife has a Volvo.'

MacMahon came forward and held out his hand. 'Good-bye.'

Elham led the way out of the sitting-room and across the

hall to the front door, which he opened. MacMahon smiled as he stepped past, Ridley merely nodded, his expression surly.

Elham closed the door and turned, to see Penelope standing in the doorway of the sitting-room. He went to speak, but checked the words because he couldn't be certain where Juana was. He hurried towards his wife. He needed to know whether he'd sounded convincing.

As he drew out on to the road, MacMahon turned right instead of left, which he would have done to return to Reckton. 'Well?'

Ridley did not try to hide his resentment. 'You went soft on him.'

'Did I?'

'You didn't follow up the fact that he was on the road just before the accident, you didn't ask him about the dinner-party and how much he'd drunk, you didn't—'

'Steve, are you too young to have heard the expression, "Softlee, softlee, catchee monkee"?'

'I've heard it, yes, but what's that to do with some poor sod getting knocked down by a car that didn't stop?'

'He's our man, isn't he?'

'That stuck out a bloody mile. Which is why I can't understand why you didn't squeeze him.'

'And immediately cause him to shut up tight, since with his experience in court he knows that the police's best friend is the accused's tongue. As of now, we've nothing that can be called proof—you know that as well as I do—so we need to keep him talking. And by letting him think he was clever and we were dumb and awed, we had him talking without ever realizing he was. How many cars were there in the garage?'

'Two.'

'A Volvo and a Metro, which probably belongs to staff.

Since both he and his wife are at home, where's the Jaguar? At a garage, being repaired?'

'We've asked to be notified about any repairs consistent with the accident and no reports have come through.'

'Quite. But take this scenario. He turns up at his usual garage and spins them a yarn of how his car got crunched. They know him as a pillar of the establishment. They'll believe him and it won't cross their minds that it could be his car we're interested in.'

'All that because he's Mister Bloody Elham?'

'Because it's an automatic reaction with ninety-nine people out of a hundred to believe that those who've really made it in life are like Cæsar's wife.'

'Who was probably a right old bag.'

Ridley, MacMahon thought, had this fatal blind spot which was fuelled by jealousy. Sooner or later, it could get him into trouble; probably, it would deny him the promotion that he deserved. 'When we get back, check the local garages for his Jag. In the meantime, we'll pay a call on the brother-in-law. I'm banking on the fact that Elham was too satisfied he pulled the wool right over our eyes to think of warning him to keep a tight mouth.'

Yew Cross consisted of several old cottages, three modern bungalows, and a pub; they were grouped around cross-roads. MacMahon braked to a halt in front of the entrance to the saloon bar of the Black Swan. 'Nip in and find out the brother-in-law's name and where he lives.'

Ridley's sense of humour took its first airing of the day. 'That requires a pint of best bitter.'

'Half a pint and you're paying.'

Ridley went inside, returned in just under five minutes. He settled in the front passenger seat. 'The woman behind the bar's not a bad bit of crackling; not bad at all. Wearing one of those dresses that make you want to drop a quid on the floor and watch her pick it up.'

'In between assessing her cleavage, did you find time to ask questions?'

'His name's Rickmore, he lives in the first house on the right down that lane, there, and he's an author.'

'We shouldn't treat him as untrustworthy just because of that.'

CHAPTER 9

Rickmore stared through one of the hall windows and convinced himself that the garden was far too sodden for him to be able to dig it, despite the fact that the day was dry. He heard a car door slam, thought it was Anne returning from the shopping, then heard a second door slam and knew it almost certainly wasn't her. He went through to the porch and after a moment two men, neither of whom he'd seen before, came round the corner of the house.

He opened the porch door as they came to a stop. 'Mr Rickmore? My name's Detective-Inspector MacMahon and this is Detective-Sergeant Ridley. Could we have a word with you?'

'Of course. Come on in.'

They entered and he pulled open the panelled door into the sitting-room, but MacMahon did not immediately move forward. 'A lovely old house, Mr Rickmore.' He stared up at the sloping ceiling which made the hall triangular in shape.

'I like it, when I can remember the ceilings are so low . . . And talking about that, keep your heads down as you go through and do mind the central beam; that's the most deadly of all.'

They settled in the sitting-room.

'I don't know whether you've yet heard,' said MacMahon

in his slow, friendly voice, 'but the man who was injured in the hit-and-run at Ailsham on Wednesday evening has died?'

'No, I hadn't. The poor devil.'

'His death obviously makes the case even more serious than it was. In fact, to put it bluntly, we'd really like to get our hands on the driver who just cleared off.'

'Yes, of course.' Rickmore's voice made it clear that he hoped they succeeded.

'So now we're trying to draw up a list of those who were on the road just before and just after the accident; that way, we may find someone who saw a car which could be the one we're looking for, while equally we'll be able to eliminate others. We've just had a word with Mr Elham and he told us he was here on Wednesday night.'

'That's right; he and his wife.'

'And he was in his Jaguar, which is . . . What model did he say it was, Steve?' MacMahon turned to Ridley, who looked uncertain.

'An XJ-S,' said Rickmore.

'Of course! A beautiful job. One needs to be a first-class driver to get the best out of that sort of machinery. Presumably, your brother-in-law's a very good driver?'

'He'll certainly agree with the assessment.'

'But you'd rather not add yours. What do they say? You can question my daughter's parentage, but not my driving skill . . . And Mr Elham also told us that when they left here, he was driving?'

'Yes, he was.'

'Neither Mr Elham nor his wife could be quite certain what the time was when they left. We need as accurate a time as possible when it comes to plotting out the cars we've had reported, so is there any chance that you can give us a sharper time than they could?'

'I don't think I can . . . Although, hang on, I've just

remembered. I went out and saw them off, then returned into the house and my wife remarked that it was just after eleven.'

'How long d'you reckon the drive back would take?'

'Quarter of an hour, give or take.'

'So he'd have arrived at his place at a quarter past eleven?'

'That's about it . . . You're trying to identify all the cars that were on the road near the time of the accident?'

'That's right.'

'Then you need to include mine. I drove over to Popham House.'

'Do you mean, after Mr and Mrs Elham had left here?'

'We found he'd left his glasses behind. We knew he'd need them the next day so tried to ring to tell him, but there wasn't any answer so I drove over.'

'What sort of time are we talking about now?'

'It must have been well after half eleven when I left here.'

'What was happening at the scene of the accident?'

'The ambulance was just pulling away.'

'That'll enable us to fix the time exactly . . . Presumably, you found Mr Elham when you reached Popham House?'

'Yes. They were outside the garage.'

'Having just arrived back?'

'I don't really know.'

'Was the Jaguar inside the garage?'

'No, it was still outside.'

'Then you can confirm that as far as you could see, it was quite undamaged?'

Rickmore hesitated. 'No, I can't.'

'Why not?'

'They'd recently bumped into something.'

'You mean, the car was damaged?'

'Slightly, yes. There was a bit of a dent in the offside wing and the light was smashed.'

'I imagine you asked what had happened?'

'I reckoned that that wouldn't have been at all popular. I don't want to make too much of this, but Terence is always very proud of his possessions and if anything of his gets damaged or refuses to work, he feels as if . . . Well, this probably sounds ridiculous, but I'm sure he feels as if he's being deliberately mocked. Can you understand what I'm trying to get at?'

'Indeed. Lots of people are like that. Steve, here, positively believes a car hates him when it won't start!'

Ridley's expression was sour.

MacMahon stood. 'Many thanks, Mr Rickmore. 'You've been a great help.'

Rickmore saw them out of the house, then shut the outside porch door and returned inside. He thought about what had been said and the impression grew that right at the end, when he'd been expressing his thanks, MacMahon had been trying to hide some emotion; a sense of triumph? But why, when he'd learned nothing pertinent to his investigations? Unless, that was . . .

'Softlee, softlee, caughtee monkee,' said MacMahon with satisfaction, as he drove on to the road and turned left.

'What a slice of luck!' said Ridley.

'Luck?'

'Sorry, masterly interrogation . . . With Elham's brother-in-law testifying against him, even the stupidest jury will have to convict.'

MacMahon changed into top. 'He obviously couldn't see the significance of the questions . . . Like I said earlier, with people in Elham's position there's an automatic and instinctive assumption which it takes a hell of a lot to destroy. But if Rickmore's as intelligent as I judge him to be, by now he'll have had to realize where our questions were leading. So will he stick with what he's told us, or will he change his tune because Elham's his brother-in-law? The answer to that will, to a large extent, depend on how they get on with each other. After meeting the two of 'em, I'd say they've very little in common.'

'They can't be too different or they wouldn't have been having dinner together.'

'Doesn't follow. Like as not, it'll have been the sisters who arranged things. The brothers-in-law just did as they were told.'

'You're being pretty cynical. For once,' Ridley added.

'My wife has a sister. Doesn't yours?'

'She's an only.'

'That you should be so lucky!'

They reached the T-junction, turned right, and came to the crossroads, where they stopped. There was no traffic coming in the opposite direction and MacMahon drove on. He enjoyed a certain sense of complacent satisfaction. Thanks to an anonymous telephone call and then to a brother-in-law too innocent and too conditioned to realize what was really happening until it was too late, Elham was now fingered for the hit-and-run. Provided nothing blew up in their faces, they ought not to have much trouble in finding the evidence to prove his guilt.

Anne, a shopping basket in her right hand, entered the house. Rickmore took the basket from her. 'Thanks, that's heavy,' she said. 'Tinned peaches were on offer and I bought three because you like them so. Incidentally, I met old Mrs Peacock in Sainsbury's and she asked how your writing was going. She seems to think you're a cross between Dickens and Zola.'

'Then obviously she hasn't read my book.'

'You'll be buried in Poets' Corner yet.'

'A consolation too delayed to be enjoyed.'

'You sound as if the world's all grey.' She walked into the kitchen. 'Have a drink and cheer up. You and Terence didn't drink us dry, did you?'

'Not quite.'

'Love, is something wrong? When I left, you were all chirpy, now you're acting like a man who's just discovered a large bill.'

He put the shopping basket down on the nearest working surface. 'While you've been out, a couple of detectives called. They're questioning people in order to try to draw up a list of who was on the road on Wednesday night at around the time of that fatal accident so that they can eliminate cars which couldn't have had anything to do with it. At least, that's what they claimed.'

'Why d'you say that?'

'I'm certain now that the real reason was solely to question me about Terence.'

'If so, why get uptight about it? He must have gone past the accident spot not long before it happened. You'll have been able to corroborate his times.'

'It was more than that.'

'More?'

'They wanted to know if I'd say anything to confirm their suspicions.'

'Suspicions about what?'

'That it was Terence who was involved.'

'My God! That's a horrible thing to say. All right, you don't like him, but really . . .'

'Whether I like or dislike him has nothing to do with it,' he said harshly.

'Yes, it has. If you didn't dislike him, you couldn't begin to think so nastily.'

'He'd had too much to drink . . .'

'And so had you, but you drove there and back and didn't knock anyone down. Thousands of men are so bloody stupid that they drink too much and then drive, but they don't knock people down.'

He said quietly: 'Do you remember what I told you when I got back? That Terence must have hit something because one wing was dented and the light was bust?'

'Well?'

'I went outside with them when they left here; the car was undamaged.'

'Oh my God! But . . . but if he'd run into someone, he'd have stopped and called for help.'

'Realizing that if he did so he'd inevitably be breathalyzed. That he'd be found to be over the limit and so he'd be accused of drunken driving, or worse; worse, as it's turned out.'

'You've got to be wrong.'

'I hope so,' he answered, without conviction.

'What do we do?'

'First tell Terence what's happened. I'll phone him now.' He left the kitchen, stood by the corner cupboard, lifted the receiver, dialled the number. There was no answer. 'They're out.'

'It's Saturday, isn't it? I've just remembered, Penny told me they were going to friends for lunch. At least, I think she did.' She was speaking disjointedly, her mind not on what she was saying.

'Then I'll try again later on.'

'Dennis, it's impossible. Terence and Penny couldn't just drive on after something like that, knowing what that could mean to the injured man . . . Oh, God, I really need that drink,' she said, in little more than a whisper.

CHAPTER 10

Titchbourne's Garage lay on the boundary of the smaller of Reckton's railway station's car parks. Originally a small, family-run business, it had been taken over twelve years previously and a four-storey administration and spares building had been erected to the right of the repair sheds. The garage held Rover, Jaguar, and Vauxhall agencies. In the forecourt, to the right of the pumps, were a number of secondhand cars for sale and amongst these there was sometimes a replica D-Type Jaguar, built by a small local specialist.

Ridley, glad to get out of the wind which had started blowing a couple of hours before and which felt as if it was coming straight in from the Arctic, went into the main shed and asked for the foreman. He was directed over to a Rover Vitesse whose bonnet was raised and into whose engine compartment two men in overalls were peering. 'If you can't get it to work, send it over to Stradley's,' he said, naming one of the three rival garages in town.

The foreman straightened up. 'What's it this time? On the bum for a rotor arm for that wreck of yours?'

'Are you offering me one?'

'Do I look that stupid?'

'No comment. How about having a chat in your office?'

'Come on, then. And maybe we can find a cup of coffee.'

They threaded their way past numerous cars being serviced and repaired, and reached a small office, built out from the wall of the shed. An electric fire was on and the interior was warm and muggy. The foreman went over to the desk and searched through a number of forms, found the one he wanted and put it by the telephone. 'I've got to ring up the owner of that Vitesse to say she can't have it back today. She'll scream. Bloody old bitch.' Two steps took him across from the desk to a small gas-ring set up on bricks, on which stood a kettle. He checked there was enough water in the kettle, lit the gas. 'So what brings you snooping about the place?' He went round the desk and gratefully slumped down on the chair behind it.

Ridley picked up a couple of loose-leaf service manuals from a second chair, put these on the floor and sat. 'Is Terence Elham one of your customers?'

'Yeah.'

'Have you got his car in for repair now?'

'Can't say off-hand.'

'Will you check?'

'When the coffee's inside me.'

The kettle boiled. The foreman reluctantly stood, went over and made two mugs of instant coffee; from the bottom drawer of the desk he brought out a half-pint bottle of milk, a jar of sugar, and a teaspoon which looked as if from time to time it was used to repair cars. 'Help yourself to what you want.'

Five minutes later he wiped his mouth with the back of his hand, belched, returned the milk and sugar to the bottom drawer, wiped the spoon on the leg of his overalls and dropped it in the drawer which he pushed shut with his foot. He reached across his desk for a thick loose-leaf file. After checking through several pages, he said: 'Elham's Jag is in for repairs.'

'What's the trouble?'

'A smashed-up offside front; wing, bonnet, wheel, radiator, suspension . . .'

'Any idea how it happened?'

'According to his wife, when they got back at night and he was driving into the garage, they ran onto some black ice. Went straight into the wall.'

'Did you collect the car?'

'With that sort of damage, d'you think it drove itself in?'

'So was it still where it had crashed when it was collected?'

'That's right; hard up against the garage wall.'

'Shit!'

'Watch the language. I've got cultured ears.'

'Have you done the repairs?'

'Can't say off-hand, but I doubt they'll have got much further than stripping down. There's a lot of work there.'

'What will have happened to the damaged bits?'

'They'll have been thrown out at the back, ready for the scrap merchant; he's maybe already collected 'em.'

'Can we find out if he has?'

The foreman closed the file with a snap. 'So what's all this in aid of?'

'Routine inquiries.'

'And my second name's Getty . . . There was a nasty hit-and-run at Ailsham recently, wasn't there?'

'It's dangerous to draw conclusions.'

'So it could have been him!' He whistled. 'A bloke in his position, eh?' He stood. 'Isn't he something to do with the law?'

'A barrister.'

'Doesn't say much for being a barrister.'

'From where I stand, there never has been.'

They left the office and went through the first shed to a yard which was littered with empty oil drums, cardboard cartons, parts of cars, and a wreck which looked as if the light van had fallen over a hundred-foot cliff. The foreman checked briefly, then said, as he kicked a badly crumpled green panel: 'All the bits and pieces are still here. You were born lucky.'

'And handsome to boot. Put 'em on one side, will you? I'll see they're collected p.d.q. . . . Can we go and have a look at the car?'

The front end of the Jaguar was on stands and two mechanics were fitting a new shock absorber. Ridley walked round to look at the nearside light pod. 'Yellow bulbs!'

'He swears blind they give a much better light. I told him they didn't and it was just a gimmick of the Frogs, but he wouldn't listen. Knows it all, that one does.'

'He doesn't know the half of it yet.'

Back at divisional HQ, MacMahon, grey-faced, obviously tired, was in his office. Ridley told him what he'd discovered.

'So he was smart enough to realize that the only way of concealing the first and incriminating damage was to overlay it with further and far more extensive damage.' MacMahon plucked at a couple of hairs on the side of his chin which his electric razor constantly missed. 'What's happening about the damaged bits?'

'I've already sent a couple of lads along to pick 'em up. I've alerted the lab and they've promised to take their fingers out. If there are any incriminating traces, they'll find 'em.'

'It'll all depend on how good a job he made of the second crash . . . Let's be pessimistic. The lab boys can't come up with anything definite enough for the court. Then Rickmore's evidence is going to be crucial.' He let go of his hairs. 'What's he going to do now he knows it's his brother-in-law's skin at risk?'

Rickmore braked to a halt in front of the garage at Popham House and the headlights of the Escort picked out the damaged brickwork. 'I wonder when that happened?' Anne said.

He ignored the question. 'D'you think we're doing the right thing, coming here now?'

'Yes, I do.'

He sighed. 'I hope you're right . . . I'm not looking forward to it.'

'You don't imagine I'm jumping with joy, do you.'

He switched off the lights and then the engine. They left the car and walked across, past the small greenhouse, to the back door. She rang the bell three times, opened the door; Elham disliked their entering by the back, but she refused to go all the way round to the front just to satisfy his social pretensions.

They passed through the deep-freeze and laundry room and entered the kitchen, which was empty but in which all the lights were on. 'Is anyone at home?' she called out. The door from the kitchen into the hall was open and they could just hear the louder notes of a Duke Ellington record. She called again and this time was answered.

They went into the blue room. The smaller of the two sitting-rooms, it possessed charm—which the larger one did not—despite the over-use of the colour which was Penelope's favourite.

Penelope was welcoming. 'What fun having you both drop in like this! I was getting so bored with my own company. Dennis, turn the record down, will you, and then you must pour us some drinks.'

She'd managed to sound as if she really were glad to see them, he thought, as he went over to the stacked disc-player and slid the volume control to its minimum setting.

'There are all the usual drinks in the cupboard, or bubbly in the fridge. Let's have that?'

He said: 'Penny, we've come to have a word with Terence. I think we ought to do that before we drink.'

'But he's upstairs, working; he never does anything else these days . . . I tell you what. We'll open one bottle and finish that before you call him down. Then he'll have to open a second one.'

'It is very important.'

'Oh, very well. I'll go and tell him to come down and be sociable. I said only the other day that when he's a Silk, I'm not having him spend all his time at home working . . .

Oh!' She touched her cheek in a quick gesture of dismay. 'I wasn't supposed to breathe a word of that to anyone. For goodness sake, do remember to forget it . . . That's rather a mix-up, isn't it?'

'Yes,' he answered.

'Penny, for God's sake, get Terence,' said Anne.

She showed both astonishment and fear and they realized that she had been trying to delay what she knew, or guessed, was going to be a painful meeting. 'All right,' she said stiffly. She stood, left.

He looked round the room. It spoke of success. The French print curtains, the Shiraz and Daghestan carpets, the authenticated Raffaelli and Dawson, the unauthenticated Modigliani, the eighteenth-century display cabinet with its lovely collection of early Staffordshire pottery, the silver, some of which was reputed to have come from the Tsar's Winter Palace . . .

Elham, followed by Penelope, entered. He said, ''Evening,' then crossed to stand in front of the fire, in the pose which came so easily to him. 'Penelope seems to think there's some sort of trouble you want to talk about?' He spoke pugnaciously, as if ready to contradict everything that was said.

'I had a couple of detectives along this morning asking questions about Wednesday evening.' Rickmore could not have missed the effect his words had had. The last, slender hope that his suspicions might, after all, be wrong, was gone.

'What questions?'

'What the time was when you left us Wednesday evening?'

'What did you answer?'

'I said that it was around eleven.'

'That's ridiculous,' snapped Penelope. 'It was only just gone ten-thirty.'

He shook his head.

'I know it was ten-thirty.'

He looked at Elham and saw that Elham's pugnacity had been replaced by fear. 'They explained why they were interested—they were trying to identify all the cars on the road before and after the accident so that they could clear all those which definitely didn't have anything to do with it. To help them, I told them I'd driven over here later on.'

'What did they say to that?' asked Elham.

'They wanted me to confirm that your Jaguar was undamaged.'

'Which you did?'

'I could hardly do that, could I? The offside wing was dented and the light pod was smashed.'

'You told them that?'

'Yes.'

'How could you?' shouted Penelope.

Rickmore didn't answer.

'Did they ask you what you meant by "dented"?' asked Elham.

'No.'

'Then you didn't explain that the whole wing was wrecked and the wheel was buckled?'

Rickmore said tightly: 'The wing was only dented and the wheel was undamaged.'

'We'd skidded on black ice and went into the corner of the garage. Both the wing and the wheel were completely wrecked.'

'The corner of the garage was undamaged.'

'Go and look at it now and see for yourself.'

'I know that when I came here Wednesday night, the corner of the garage was untouched.'

'And I'm telling you, it wasn't.'

There was a silence, which became more painful for each of them the longer it lasted. Rickmore finally broke it. 'Terence, was it the Jaguar which hit that man?'

'No,' replied Elham violently.

'Then why does it matter quite so much to you exactly when the garage was damaged?'

'Because if the police believe you're telling the facts, they may start beginning to suspect me of having been the driver.'

'If you're innocent, you'll soon clear yourself.'

'For God's sake, how can you be so stupid? Don't you know that acquittal and innocence are two different things.'

'That's one hell of a thing for someone like you to say.'

'D'you think innocence has a shining ring of truth about it that can't be missed? D'you believe that old saw; Witnesses may lie, but circumstances cannot? Are you so naive that you accept that the police are more interested in a man's innocence than their own clear-up rate?'

'But you're saying . . .'

'I'm saying that if you persist in telling the police what you've just said here, they're going to suspect me; and once that happens, every piece of evidence that is turned up will be carefully angled towards confirming my guilt.'

'You do realize something, don't you? The man who was knocked down has died. Doesn't that mean something to you?'

'I had nothing to do with his death.'

'When you left our place, you weren't in a fit state to drive.'

'No? I'd had no more to drink than you, yet you drove over here. Were you in a fit state to drive?'

'I . . . If I'd knocked someone down, I'd have stopped to do what I could for the poor devil.'

'Are you so certain?'

'What d'you mean?'

'Would you be seized by quite so much righteousness if it weren't someone else who was involved, it was you?'

'The principle's the same.'

'Principles are never the same for oneself.'

'That's an extraordinary thing for you to say.'

'It's an extraordinary fact that you liberals can never . . .' He stopped. He ran the back of his hand across his forehead. 'This is quite ridiculous. We're arguing and becoming quite heated, yet there's nothing to argue about . . . I am not trying to say the police would ever deliberately set out to inculpate a man they know to be innocent. What I am pointing out is that they're human, grossly overworked, and unfortunately judged by results. So if the evidence in a case appears to point to one conclusion, they're sometimes over-ready to accept that conclusion and do not exert themselves to find out if it might, after all, be incorrect.

'You can see what that means here. They're searching for a car that was near the cricket ground at the relevant time and which bears signs of damage compatible with an impact with the victim. The moment they find such a car, they'll tend to concentrate on that one to the exclusion of all others . . . Because of what you've already told them, they're bound to think it could be my car they're looking for. So they'll have checked with all the garages and will have found that the Jaguar is being repaired in Titchbourne's. They'll have examined the damage and inevitably have come to the conclusion that it is far greater than would have been sustained in the accident. But because, by now, they'll have come to the conclusion it could have been my car, they're going to claim I deliberately crashed my car into the garage after the accident in order to hide the signs of damage resulting from it. So if you insist, wrongly, in maintaining that when you were here the Jaguar was only lightly damaged and the garage wall was untouched, their false accusations are going to appear to be corroborated.'

Rickmore said very slowly: 'The wing was only dented, the wheel was not buckled, the garage was untouched.'

'You filthy swine!' Penelope shouted.

'I . . . I have to tell the truth.'

'Hypocrite.'

He flushed. 'I do happen to believe that justice means justice for everyone . . .'

'Justice? You don't give a damn for justice.'

'Penny . . .' began Elham.

'If you won't tell him, I will.' She faced Rickmore, her expression ugly with hatred. 'All you're interested in is in getting your own back on Terence.'

'Doing what, for God's sake?'

'Getting your own back because he's a success and you're a failure. The police didn't come to you, you deliberately went to them and tried to implicate Terence with your filthy lies.'

Anne stood. 'I think we'd better leave.'

'Then go.'

Elham gestured with his hands, looked at Rickmore, then at his wife. He turned away, shoulders slumped.

Anne and Rickmore left the sitting-room and went through the hall, the kitchen, and deep-freeze room to the yard. They climbed into the Escort and, for once, the engine started at the first turn of the key.

He drove slowly, his thoughts jumbled and painful. All his thinking life, he'd accepted that for a country to have freedom, it must have justice. Justice depended on just laws and people who observed their duty to obey them. Each time such a duty was dishonoured, justice suffered and therefore freedom was imperilled . . . But could Elham be right? Was there for every individual a line which drew the boundary between duty and self-preservation? Could he, hand on heart, honestly affirm that in Elham's position he would have done his duty at no matter what cost to himself?

Anne said: 'It was Terence who hit the man, wasn't it?'

'Yes.'

'Oh God!' She put her forearm on the back of his seat so

that she could touch his neck, needing the comfort of physical contact. 'What's going to happen?'

He shook his head. He knew only one thing. He would do his duty, which was to tell the truth, no matter what this cost in emotional terms.

CHAPTER 11

Monday was dry and fine, with only good weather clouds; but for the temperature, it might have been the beginning of spring.

Rickmore stared at the cuttings from the French agent which had arrived from Paris by the morning's post. Each cutting contained a reference to Teerson's Products and was presumed to have appeared in response to the newsletters which Rickmore sent out; as such, the cuttings were held to provide an indication of how effective his newsletters were and it was his job to translate the relevant passages into English so that they could be read by the directors. Had he, as he'd claimed when he'd applied for the position of PRO, been fluent in French it would not have been a difficult task; as it was, it was one that invariably taxed his ingenuity and patience. But he'd learned to work on the principle that if the references were never less than complimentary, no one would ever bother to check the translations.

The intercom buzzed and he pressed down the appropriate switch. 'Yes, Daphne?' He shared his secretary with Advertising. She was dumpy, yet dressed as if she had the figure of a model. Parkes had once asured him that she was a girl with potential. Since then, he'd always considered Parkes rather odd, even for someone in Advertising.

'There are two gentlemen who'd like to see you, Mr Rickmore. They're detectives.'

'OK, send them in.' That would start the rumour mills turning, he thought.

MacMahon and Ridley were shown into the room by Daphne, who was wearing a pleated skirt in a bright tartan which added inches to her already generous waist. She tried to stay to learn at least a little of what was going on, but he thanked her in a way that left her no option but to go.

MacMahon, he thought, wasn't looking fit, Ridley appeared aggressive. They shook hands with careful formality, then he set two chairs in front of the desk.

'I'm sorry to bother you during working hours,' said MacMahon.

'As far as I'm concerned, don't apologize.'

MacMahon smiled. 'Even so, we won't keep you for long . . . When we had a word with you before, you mentioned that on Wednesday night Mr Elham and his wife had dinner with you and that he left his spectacles at your place. You tried to ring him to say so, but couldn't get through, so you drove them over. Have I got that right?'

'Yes, you have.'

'Will you tell us again, as exactly as you can, what happened when you arrived?'

He described the events, his voice hard because there was no way now of avoiding the knowledge of what might be the consequences of his words.

'I'd like to get a mental picture of this dent in the wing. How deep would you say it was?'

'I don't think I can make a reliable estimate.'

'Why not?'

'One needs some sort of yardstick and I didn't have one.'

'Fair enough. Then how would you describe it in general terms?'

'Not very large and not very deep.'

'You place it on the turn of the wing, some way back from the lights. And the bonnet was untouched?'

'That's right.'

'This was night-time, but the outside lights of the garage were switched on. Do they give a reasonable light?'

'A good one.'

'Then if the wing had been buckled and torn, instead of being merely dented, and the bonnet had been crumpled, you'd have noticed the fact.'

'Yes.'

'Did you look at the offside wheel?'

'Not specifically, no.'

'You can't say if it was badly buckled?'

'Not directly. But if it had been, I'd have thought I'd have noticed it.'

'Was the corner of the garage in any way damaged?'

'No.'

'You are quite certain about that?'

'Positive.'

'Then that, I think, is all we need to know for the moment.' MacMahon stood. 'I'd like to thank you for being so frank. It can't have been very easy for you.'

'It hasn't been.'

'I hope it'll help if I tell you that you've done the right thing.'

After they'd left, Rickmore resumed his seat. MacMahon said he'd done the right thing. But had he? Could consequences be ignored? Yes, he decided; they could and must be when justice demanded that.

An hour and a half later, Ridley walked into MacMahon's office. 'You're looking rotten,' he said, as he came to a stop in front of the desk.

'Just tired.'

'Are you quite sure? Wouldn't it be an idea if . . .'

'I am quite sure.' MacMahon pulled himself upright.

'If you say so . . . I've had a bloke from the lab on the

phone. Damage to the various bits is consistent with running fairly hard into a brick wall. They've recovered traces of brick dust and want to know if we'd like 'em to run comparison tests with samples taken from the wall?'

'Not much point to that. It's Elham who claims to have rammed the wall.'

'That's what I reckoned . . . One interesting bit of news. At one point of the offside wing, the force of the impact split and folded the metal back on itself, forming a pocket that was never in direct contact with the wall. The lab's managed to raise an impression on the paintwork inside this and they say that in their opinion the impression was formed by an article of clothing of woollen texture.'

'The sweater the victim was wearing?' said MacMahon, his voice suddenly sharp.

'They're testing. But the chap I spoke to warned me that the impression was blurred and, because of the deformation of the metal, distorted. He said the odds were against their being able to make a unique comparison.'

MacMahon began to tap on the desk. 'Then at best it'll be no more than corroborative evidence and a good defence lawyer could probably turn it inside out.'

'If it's on its own, maybe. But if it's in there with other evidence, the jury will get the right idea.'

'Provided there's some central, unshakable fact on which to hang all this.'

'Rickmore's evidence, surely?'

MacMahon stopped tapping. 'What about the sliver of glass—did the lab mention that?'

'Similar to the control glass, but the crime sample was too small for any definite comparison.'

'I suppose if we'd given them half the headlamp glass, they'd have shouted for the other half before they'd commit themselves . . . Every time defence counsel makes an expert witness look like a wally, the lab boys expend a bit more energy on defending their backs and a bit less on doing their job . . . We've not yet checked out the dirt forced into the victim's clothes, have we?'

'There's not been time.'

'There never is. Find out if there've been any repairs carried out recently on the house or garage; if there have been, get samples of the brick and wood. And find out if the Elhams employ full-time staff. If they do . . .'

'They will. Too bloody lazy to do the work themselves.'

MacMahon leaned back in his chair. 'I've said it before and I'm about to say it again. If you go on carrying around that chip on your shoulder, sooner or later you'll end up in right royal trouble.'

'What chip?'

'Your resentment of anybody who has more than you.'

Ridley's expression became sullen.

'No one ever will invent a society where there aren't have-nots as well as haves.'

'So the haves aren't complaining.'

MacMahon sighed. Ridley would never understand. 'If any staff were around on Wednesday night, find out what they heard or saw. And try to discover if we're ever going to be told whether the dead man's dabs are on file. It's four days now since we requested a search.'

'I got on to 'em earlier and was given a lecture. The present computer is so slow that it can take up to ten days to go through its database of three hundred and fifty thousand prints. But some genius is working on a new computer that'll cut the time down to one day.'

'Always jam tomorrow,' said McMahon.

Juana opened the door and Ridley introduced himself. He then explained what he wanted, speaking very simply because he'd never overcome the teachings of his mother that all foreigners were stupid. Juana was worried, since neither the señor nor the señora was in the house to guide her as to what to do, but Ridley could be charming when bothered to take the trouble and soon she had forgotten her worries and she asked him into the kitchen for a cup of tea.

While he was eating a second wholemeal biscuit, a man came into the kitchen and was introduced by Juana as her husband, who worked in the garden. That, thought Ridley, was fairly obvious; Cavajals had brought part of it in with him.

'Have you had any repairs done recently?' he asked.

Cavajals looked at his wife, who spoke more English than he did. 'You wish to know the garage?' she asked.

He shook his head. 'No, not just for the moment. Have any repairs been done, to a window or a door maybe? Has anything been made or altered?'

'There is the . . .' She came to a stop.

'The what?'

'I do not know how is called.'

'Is it part of the house?'

She shook her head. 'It is . . .' She stopped again. Then she said, very impatient at being unable to express herself clearly: 'Please to come with me.'

He followed her out to the yard and the garden immediately beyond this and she showed him a cold-frame, newly put together by her husband—if he understood her correctly —from a kit supplied by a local firm. Her husband had had to alter one corner. Her husband was a very clever man with a hammer, saw, or screwdriver . . . Yes, he had had to do a bit of sawing. And because it had been cold and the Jaguar had been out, he had done it inside the garage . . .

The floor of the garage was concreted and in one place it had cracked; in this crack—which, she said, was about where her husband had worked—was a sprinkling of saw-dust. He used an old and battered tablespoon, found on a workbench, to lift out the sawdust and drop it into a plastic bag she brought him.

They returned to the kitchen. Cavajals had left and the coffee in their mugs was cold. Ridley said he didn't mind cold coffee, but she emptied both their mugs and switched on the electric kettle.

He asked her about Wednesday night once she'd made fresh coffee and was seated at the kitchen table. She explained that they'd been in their house which was beyond and behind the garage.

'What was the time when you went to bed?'

As usual, they'd gone to bed early. Because he didn't understand the television, her husband only watched sport and if she tried to watch anything else he became annoyed, so they seldom stayed up at night.

'Did you hear the Elhams return?'

'They come back, yes.'

'Have you any idea what that time was?'

She shrugged her shoulders.

'Was it soon after you'd gone to bed?'

'Not soon. Miguel is asleep. I could not be sleepy and I read.'

'Have a guess what the time was.'

She was silent for so long that he thought she wasn't going to answer, then she said: 'I think it was a good time after eleven.'

'Did another car arrive after them?'

'I stop the reading and turn the light off. Then it come.'

'Was it here for long?'

'Not long. And after it go, there is a crash. I think something bad is happened. But there is no more noise.'

'Can you describe what kind of a noise it was?'

'I think was the señor to hit the garage.'

'And this was definitely after the other car had left?'

'Please?'

He repeated the question and she confirmed that the crash had been after and not before.

They were, Ridley thought with deep satisfaction, gradually tightening the noose around Elham's cowardly neck; soon, they'd pull it tight.

CHAPTER 12

Rickmore left the garage and walked towards the garden gate. Even on a winter's day, Oak Tree Cottage was attractive. Not because the proportions were good—they weren't; the cottage was unreservedly boxy—but because three centuries had made it as much part of the countryside as the large and majestic oak whose upper branches could be seen to the right and beyond. He sometimes wondered who'd been the original occupants and what kind of a life they'd led. A thought which other authors had exploited . . .

As he opened the gate, he noted that one of the upright slats was still loose and needed nailing back; he assured himself that he'd do that at the first opportunity, knowing that he'd put it off for as long as he possibly could. For him, nails bent and hammers missed. Anne had described his carpentry as Mack Sennett comedy.

Anne entered the hall from the sitting-room and he kissed her.

'Well! It's some time now since you've been romantic on your return from work. Have you had a rise?' She studied his face and her tone changed. 'No, it's not like that at all, is it?'

He hung his lined mackintosh on one of the hooks on the wall to the right of the porch door. 'The two detectives called at the office. I confirmed all I'd told them before, so now I'm left wondering if I'm a rotten bastard.'

'Do you think you are?'

'More to the point, do you?'

Her gaze never left him, her high-boned face expressing conviction, but also sadness. 'Not if you truly believe you had to do what you've done.'

'He is your brother-in-law.'

'Does that alter the principle?'

'Of course not. But it must affect the light in which other people will see my actions.'

'You're worried by what people will think?'

'I don't give a damn about them if I know I've done the right thing.'

'Have you?'

He managed a wry smile. 'Hasn't that brought us round in a circle?'

'What is it, Dennis? D'you want me to agree that you had to do it?'

He was worried by her tone, but tried not to show that. 'I suppose I would like confirmation that my motives for telling the truth are as pure and high-minded as I've been assuring myself.'

'And not as mean and contemptible as Penny suggested?'

'Ouch!'

She stepped forward and kissed him again. 'Listen, my love. If the whole world said that your motives were utterly sordid and despicable, and you assured me they weren't, I'd know the whole world was wrong. You're an idealist and if that sometimes means you're difficult to live with, I don't care. I wouldn't change you for anyone.'

He hugged her. 'I'm a very lucky man.'

'Quite right.'

'No false modesty?'

'None whatsoever.' After a moment, she disengaged herself. 'I'll make some coffee.'

He followed her to the doorway of the kitchen, leaned

against the side. He watched her fill the coffee machine with water and not for the first time wondered how two sisters could be so different in character.

Ridley was late and he hurried up to his room, which was smaller than MacMahon's but which he did have to himself —something that rarely happened in the older stations. He checked the desk top, but there was no ironic message asking him if he'd be good enough to go to the DI's room if and when he had a moment to spare. So MacMahon wouldn't know he'd been late . . . The telephone rang and the caller was Mrs MacMahon. Her husband had been unwell during the night, the doctor had seen him and had called for an ambulance, and he was now in hospital; the hospital doctors seemed to think he might have suffered a slight heart attack. So he would not be in to work for a while. She didn't say so, but she was obviously worried sick that perhaps he never would be back.

Ridley used the internal telephone to tell the divisional superintendent that the DI was ill, then the outside one to give the same message to the detective chief superintendent at county HQ. He was informed that a relief DI would be sent down as soon as possible, but because the Force was so short staffed at the moment, this might take time; until then, he was acting DI.

He went through to the DI's room, ostensibly to find out if any of the morning's mail needed urgent attention, in reality to see how the room fitted him. It fitted him like a glove.

The laboratory assistant telephoned at four fifty-six on Wednesday. By then, Ridley, while no less confident of his own abilities, was prepared to admit that the job of detective-inspector was a more difficult one than he'd supposed. Especially when the detective-constables couldn't—or wouldn't—carry out their orders exactly as he wanted them carried out.

The assistant said: 'Both the control and crime samples of sawdust were softwood, treated against rotting with some fungicide. As you'll know with sawdust, there's seldom much hope of a positive identification and the best we can do here is to say that the samples are similar. There's no chance of specifically identifying the fungicide used.'

'Is that all?'

'What more do you want?'

He wanted a positive identification, but obviously was not going to get one. He thanked the woman and rang off. Every time, it was the same. The two samples were similar, but not uniquely so. They'd still not one single piece of unshakable evidence to complement Rickmore's testimony . . . That left only one way of going about things. Pressure Elham until he admitted his guilt. MacMahon had steadfastly denied that this was the way, but he'd joined the Force in the days when a policeman metaphorically doffed his helmet to the gentry. All that gibberish about softlee, softlee, catchee monkee. A smokescreen, to try to obscure the fact that he could not shake himself free of his instinctive deference . . .

Ridley looked at his wristwatch. When would the old bastard get back from London? Certainly by eight. So hit him then, at the end of his working day, when he'd be too tired to be fully alert mentally. Force him to admit that it had been his car which had slammed into the as-yet unidentified man . . .

Elham had hired a Granada, since the Jaguar would not be ready until the following day. He turned into his drive and saw, with sharp annoyance, that a dirt-stained car was blocking his way into the garage.

Penelope met him in the hall. 'The police are here,' she

said in a low voice. He experienced immediate tension and fear. 'Pull yourself together,' she said fiercely.

He briefly wondered how he could have been married to her for years, yet never have realized that when necessary she could be as hard as nails.

'If you don't tell them anything, they can't prove anything.'

Had she no idea how the police worked; how they uncovered one small piece of evidence here, one small piece there, then stitched them all together to prove the accused's guilt?

'They tried to question me. I told them their suspicions were disgusting and libellous.'

Slanderous, he automatically thought. Into his mind there came the image of the man suddenly appearing in the car's headlights . . . A few seconds only, but which now threatened the whole of his future life . . .

'Show some backbone.'

He'd said the same thing, more elegantly phrased, to men he'd defended and whose servile attitudes had virtually been admissions of guilt. He was learning it was not so easy when one was the accused . . .

She dug her fingers into his arm, so tightly that even through the thick, good quality cloth and the sleeve of his shirt, the grip was almost painful. 'Make them believe you.'

He went into the blue sitting-room. Ridley briefly introduced Detective-Constable Cricks. Elham wondered where MacMahon was and wished he'd come instead of Cricks; MacMahon had been pleasant and understanding.

'I want to go over a few points again,' said Ridley, his manner openly antagonistic. 'On Wednesday evening, you left your brother-in-law's house at around eleven o'clock . . .'

'At around ten-thirty,' he corrected.

'Mr Rickmore says that it quite definitely was eleven.'

'He is mistaken.'

'Your maid agrees that you returned some time after eleven.'

'Juana? I fear she's not a good time-keeper, as we soon discovered after she started working for us.' He was surprised how easily confident he managed to sound; just the right amount of casual indifference as to how his answers were received; a man of consequence, naturally willing to assist the police, but certainly not to be browbeaten . . .

Penelope confirmed what her husband had said, in a way that sharply exacerbated Ridley's resentment, since she sounded condescending. Because of this, he made the mistake of claiming too much. He said that the forensic laboratory had definitely concluded that the imprinted pattern on the damaged wing from the Jaguar had been made by the dead man's sweater . . .

Elham, knowing that the detective-sergeant could not be telling the truth—had he been, he'd have come to arrest, not question—understood that the other had thought to panic him into an admission. The knowledge gave him confidence. He asked what proof there was that the impression had not been implanted at some time after the car had been taken to the garage—could the police prove constant reference? What gave the so-called impression its unique quality . . .'

Angrily, Ridley introduced the sliver of glass. This had been identified as coming from the headlamp of the Jaguar. This time, Elham asked only one question. Was the laboratory prepared to say that it had come from the headlamp of the Jaguar and could not possibly have come from any other car? When Ridley did not answer, he ostentatiously shrugged his shoulders as he would have done if addressing a jury.

Ridley spoke with even greater antagonism. What about the sawdust found in the victim's clothing? Had it been proved beyond question, Elham asked quietly, that the sawdust was similar in every respect, uniquely similar in every respect, to the sawdust found in the garage? Ridley said that the car Daley had seen had had yellow lights. So, remarked Elham, did every French car on the roads. But perhaps there had been something about those yellow lights which positively identified them as British, not French?

When Ridley left, his expression was bitter.

As they heard the car leave, Penelope said: 'You were really marvellous!' Her surprise was less flattering than her words.

He went out to the drinks cupboard and poured himself a whisky and her a Campari. He noticed that his hands were shaking. He was like an actor who'd suffered stage fright right up to the moment of appearance, yet had acted superbly as the adrenalin flowed, then suffered badly from reaction the moment the curtain dropped.

He returned to the sitting-room and handed her a glass.

'You completely silenced the insolent man!'

As he stared at her, he noticed several small and wholly immaterial things, as often happened in a moment of mental stress. She was using a different shade of lipstick and was wearing the ear-rings he'd given her the previous Christmas; there were lines about her mouth that hadn't been there before; her dress was tight and her breasts were well outlined, breasts which should have summoned passion . . .

'Terence, have you been struck dumb?'

'No.'

'Then why don't you say something? Why are you still looking so miserable?'

'You obviously don't understand.'

'I understand you sent that man packing, with his tail between his legs.'

He sat down on the nearest chair, drank. 'I'm worried because they've found out so much.'

'They've discovered nothing of importance. Every time he tried to claim they had, you showed he was lying.'

'It's true I could knock each piece of evidence independently. But when they're all put together, they're good enough to strengthen the central evidence. And when that's strengthened, it in turn strengthens them.' He finished the whisky, stood, saw she had not yet touched her drink, left the room and refilled his glass. When he returned, he stood in front of the fire instead of sitting. 'Take the imprint they've found on the wing. Obviously, it's not good enough to prove that a specific sweater must have made it. But it fits in with the central evidence which says that it was my car which hit the man; one moves on from there to the fact that if it was my car, it's probably the dead man's sweater which made it. And if there's other evidence which fits in in the same way, then before long all these pieces of evidence cease to be separate but become part of the pattern. In other words, they corroborate the central evidence—Dennis's.'

'He can't do it to you,' she said fiercely.

'Perhaps, after what you said to him the other night, it's become more of a pleasure than a duty.'

'I was terribly upset.'

'But will he allow for that.'

'My God, he is my brother-in-law, isn't he?'

'And also a man of principles.'

'What's that to do with it? He can't do it to us. You've got to talk to him and make him understand.'

'Since when has any liberal ever understood the nature of the world he lives in?'

CHAPTER 13

Seated in his office, Rickmore knew a painful embarrassment. Elham seemed to have lost all sense of self-respect.

'Can't you realize what it would mean to Penelope and me?'

'Yes, of course, but . . .'

'If you tell the court exactly the same as you've told the police, I'm bound to be found guilty. At worst, I'll be jailed, at best I'll receive a suspended sentence; either way, I'll be disbarred.'

'We've been through all this before . . .'

'I'll be out of work and unqualified to do anything else. For God's sake, think what it would mean to Penelope, even if you've never bothered to consider what it would mean to me.'

'Not considered it? I've not thought about much else . . . All I'm doing is telling the truth.'

'And you think it's right to do that no matter what happens to the family?'

'But the truth . . .'

'Do you hate me that much?'

'For God's sake, I don't hate you at all.'

Elham leaned forward until he was sitting on the edge of the chair. 'Suppose I admitted it was the Jaguar, but I swore by everything I hold sacred that I had absolutely no chance of avoiding him; that even if I hadn't had a single drink all night, it wouldn't have made the slightest difference? What then?'

'How could that alter the need to tell the truth?'

'You'd still think it right to see me ruined over something over which I'd no control?'

'You should have stopped the car after it happened.'

'There was an oncoming car and that reached the man within seconds.'

'You didn't know at the time whether seconds might have made the difference between life and death.'

Elham said, not realizing that he had virtually abandoned the fiction that his last few questions had been hypothetical: 'What gives you the right to set yourself up as the judge?'

'I'm not.'

'Do you imagine that there's another man in the whole country who'd betray his own family like this?'

Rickmore said desperately: 'I don't know; I just don't bloody know what any other man would do in this God-awful situation. I only know what I've got to do.'

'Got to?'

'Yes.'

Elham stood. He stared down at Rickmore, his expresion strained. 'If . . . if I offered you ten thousand pounds?'

Rickmore tried to keep his contemptuous anger under control. 'If the offer was made to get me to change my evidence, I'd tell you just what to do with it.'

Elham's shoulders slumped. He turned, went over to the door, then suddenly swung round. His voice was shrill. 'Every man has his price. I just wonder what yours is?'

Because of the time of day, the train arrived at Charing Cross and not Cannon Street. Elham left the first-class carriage and walked along the platform to the ticket barrier. He showed his season ticket and went through. He felt as if part of him was standing aside and observing, with clinical detachment, his ever-quickening advance towards disaster.

He looked up at the large overhead clock. Half past eleven. He should have been in court, but earlier he'd telephoned Arnold and told him to see if Trent could take the watching brief. He suddenly knew an overwhelming pity for himself. Why? Why had it happened to him?

Lucy, he suddenly thought. She couldn't offer him escape, but she could give him temporary forgetfulness. He turned and went through one of the exits to the pavement and the taxi-rank.

The taxi went through Admiralty Arch and down The Mall. His thoughts raced ahead. Because of all that had happened, it was days since he'd phoned her, let alone seen her. She must have become worried. So she'd be even more passionate than usual and in the white heat of that passion, he'd be able to forget . . . Defining what he'd forget made him remember it. He stared through the glass partition, silently urging the driver to greater speed.

The taxi arrived at Cuthbertson Road and drew up outside No. 22. He paid, crossed to the steps, climbed these, pressed the bell for the top flat. The speaker crackled into life and a man said: 'Who is it?'

Stupidly, he checked that he had pressed the button for the top floor.

'Who is it, then?'

He knew that she employed male models (better never to wonder, remembering those sculptures, what pose she required) and decided the speaker must be one. 'Is Lucy there?'

'Yeah. So now who are you?'

'Terence.'

As he waited, he wondered how old the model was.

'She says she's busy.'

'But I must see her.'

There was a long silence. He pressed the bell again. This time, Lucy answered him. 'Terry, go away. I can't see you.'

'I'm in trouble; terrible trouble. I need you desperately.'

The man spoke again. 'Look, Terry-boy, the lady doesn't want to know you any more. Got it?'

He stood there for over a minute, absurdly waiting for her to tell him that it had all been a silly mistake and to come straight up . . . Finally, he turned and went down the steps, feeling sick and old. It did not occur to him that it had been shame which had made her refuse to meet him.

Betty returned to the clerks' room and sat behind her desk, but did nót immediately resume work on the Statement of Claim. 'It was Mr Elham who came in just now. He looks really terrible.'

Arnold stared at her over the tops of the half-moon glasses he wore when his eyes were tired. 'What exactly do you mean?'

'I think he must be ill. Either that or something terrible has happened.'

He wondered if she was being stupid.

'You know, if you come to think about it, he's not been his usual self for days.'

There was some truth in that.

'D'you think he's worried about taking Silk?'

'Of course not,' he replied sharply.

'Then maybe it's something which has happened at home. I mean, with a wife like his, anything . . .'

'Shall we leave his private life private? Suppose you get on with the work.'

'All right, all right.' She liked him, but that didn't stop her finding him, at times, a pompous old fool. She wound a sheet of paper into the typewriter and typed in the name of counsel, the case, and the name of instructing solicitors. She looked across at Arnold and saw that his high, greasy forehead was creased, as it always was when he was worried. He could huff and puff as much as he liked, but Mr Elham's wife was a bitch . . .

Arnold tried to concentrate on the fees' book he was bringing up to date, but his mind kept returning to what she'd just said. Was Mr Elham either ill or desperately worried over something?

After a while, he left and went along to Elham's room and with even greater disquiet saw that Elham was not working but was slumped back in his chair, staring into space, his expression that of a man under intolerable pressure. 'Mr Trent appeared for your clients; everything went smoothly.' Elham turned and looked directly at him and he was shocked by the expression now in the other's eyes. He blurted out: 'Is something wrong?' Then he added: 'Is there anything I can do?'

Arnold, at the age of four days, was named Thomas Arnold as he had been found on St Thomas's day in Arnold Street. Since the small wooden box had been left at one of the rear entrances of the Clarence Hertchwitz Memorial Hospital, he should, perhaps, have considered himself lucky.

The orphanage in which he'd spent his early life had been well run, but his years there had been filled with dull despair. His nature was of the kind that needed a deep, lasting, and particular relationship if it were to be fulfilled and this he failed to find; the staff were too busy, and trained to be too egalitarian, to give more to him than to the others in their care, and because he was shy and solitary he failed to strike up any deep friendships with his peers.

He'd almost married when he was twenty-two. But a fortnight before the wedding, the woman, seven years older in time, seventy years older in experience, had met a merchant seaman from Glasgow who'd offered her Nirvana and, despite all her experience, she'd gone off with him. The humiliation of this had hurt deeply, although he eventually realized that in fact she would have made him very unhappy. He never contemplated marriage again and very seldom went out with women, even though he was not a homosexual; he usually felt uncomfortable in their presence.

His first job, gained through the influence of one of the governors of the orphanage, had been as an old-fashioned office boy in chambers which had been headed by a QC who'd been as successful as he was objectionable. The QC had died suddenly, the head clerk had retired, and he'd been promoted to assistant clerk. Several years later the building had been redeveloped and the chambers had split up; he'd found work in another set, almost at the same time as Elham joined them as a pupil.

As he was given more responsibility, so he discovered that not only did he enjoy the work, he was very good at it. Solicitors liked him, probably because he treated them with considerable respect and their egos were always finely tuned when dealing with the senior branch of the law; barristers liked him because they found they could trust his judgement; his judgement was good because he had a natural flair for bargaining which seldom let him down and he could tell how high he could demand a brief be marked before instructing solicitors rebelled. At the same time, he also developed an instinct which suggested how successful any barrister was likely to be.

He'd soon judged that the highest posts in the judiciary were not beyond Elham's reach. So he'd carefully hitched himself to Elham's star. And strangely, although this had been a material decision—as Elham's status grew, so would his—he'd found that relationship for which he'd been searching all his life. He didn't know what Elham felt about that, but he didn't care. It was sufficient for him that he could be a part of his life and climb the ladder in his shadow.

So he'd been shocked and frightened when Elham told him all that had happened; so shocked and frightened that for the rest of the day he'd been unable to do any work and Betty had fussed, believing him to be sickening for the 'flu.

He left chambers sharp on five—a unique event—and caught the tube to Clapham. A ten-minute walk brought him to the house in which he'd lodged for the past seven years. He let himself in, called a greeting to the landlady in the kitchen, and went up the stairs to his two rooms. He settled in the armchair in the sitting-room and stared at the blank screen of the large television set he'd bought himself the previous year . . . Desperately, he tried to think clearly. Because he was totally unconcerned with the morality of Elham's actions, the question was not whether he should try to help, but how. How, in God's name, to save Elham from being ruined by his brother-in-law? Because he'd never met Rickmore, he had to imagine him in a villainous guise in order to hate him the more. If only he could be knocked down and killed in another road accident before he gave his evidence in court! Would it be any good travelling down to Reckton and seeing Rickmore and pleading with him not to testify? But Elham had said that Rickmore was motivated by a sense of duty and therefore it was impossible to talk sense with him. Then how to silence the prosecution's main witness? Or reduce the value of his testimony to the point where it was no longer strong enough to support the circumstantial evidence . . .

Frustration squeezed his mind. He longed to sacrifice himself, yet could not discover how. He stood and crossed the room to the small cupboard beyond the television set and brought out a bottle of whisky and a glass. It was his invariable custom to have one whisky before his supper. Tonight, he had three. And because he was unaccustomed to so much alcohol, his mind began to wander, to twist and turn . . . And suddenly he realized that there was one way in which the value of Rickmore's evidence could be fatally weakened . . .

He paced the floor, the alcohol no longer confusing his thoughts but seemingly sharpening and polishing them. Two years back, a brief had come into chambers from solicitors working for a trust which helped people in need.

The scent of charity had kept the markings low and so the brief had gone to Vernay. The trial had not been a long one and Vernay had been extraordinarily lucky with one of the main prosecution witnesses, but the accused, Dean, had believed he owed his freedom to brilliance rather than luck (a common mistake with those who, to their complete astonishment, were acquitted). Dean had come up to them outside the courtroom (Elham had not been in court that day, so Arnold had been free to accompany Vernay to see how he was shaping) and had said: 'If ever I can do either of you gents a good turn, just ask. That's all, just ask and I'll come running.' Later, Vernay had said that they must remember the offer in case either of them wanted to go in for burglary. At the time, Arnold had disapproved of such levity. Now he remembered the words in a very different light . . .

CHAPTER 14

The phone rang and Ridley picked up the receiver. 'DI,' he said, no longer aware that he had promoted himself.

'It's Dabs here. We've an identification for you, reference seventeen six stroke nine.'

That was the hit-and-run victim. So MacMahon had been right when he'd surmised that the victim had been engaged in some criminal activity. Ridley picked up a ballpoint pen. 'Shoot.'

'Richard Tamworth. One conviction, for indecent assault.'

'A sex merchant!'

'His last known address is twenty-six, Updyke Road, Evenham. But that's pretty old, so it may not be worth much.'

'You'll send us a copy of his file?'

'Of course.'

'By the way, he's died.'

'Then I'll transfer him to the gone and unlamented section.'

After replacing the receiver, Ridley stared down at the sheet of paper on which he'd written the name and address. It was now possible to postulate two facts. That Tamworth's disappearance hadn't been reported because whoever knew he'd disappeared also knew the possible reason for his disappearance and was too ashamed, or scared, to draw attention to it. That the reason for his sudden and fatal appearance on a section of road where there were no homes nearby had been that he'd committed an offence of a sexual nature and had been fleeing pursuit . . . Yet against this last was the fact that there'd been no report of any such incident on the Wednesday night . . .

Behind the desk was a large-scale map of the county, with the divisional boundaries marked in red. He found Ailsham cricket ground and the double bend in the road just south of it. Where could Tamworth have come from? Somewhere where there were potential victims. The countryside was populated, but except in the villages the houses were fairly well apart. That could appeal to a sex criminal, since he was less likely to be disturbed and caught; on the other hand, it meant far fewer potential victims from which to choose and a much greater risk of being noted. Ridley visually examined the surrounding countryside, searching for somewhere that would have attracted a sex criminal . . . Hacksley House. Once a rich man's mansion, now a geriatric hospital. Nurses worked in hospitals and nurses' hostels were frequently targets. A long shot, but not impossibly so . . .

He drove the four miles to Hacksley House and parked against the raised flowerbed in the centre of the turning circle immediately in front of the portico. He climbed out of the car and looked up at the large Queen Anne mansion. Once, just one man had owned all that, together with the park which stretched right round it; dozens of servants had catered to his every whim. Ridley knew a brief satisfaction at the thought that the man and his descendants had been dispossessed.

The matron had an office on the ground floor, to the rear of the house. She was a tall, firmly proportioned woman, quiet in manner, with a face which expressed both strength and compassion. She showed no surprise when he explained what he was looking for and he was pretty certain that after a working lifetime in nursing there was little that could surprise her.

Her voice was well pitched and brisk. 'There were no official reports of any incident on that Wednesday night.'

'There weren't.' He was disappointed, but not surprised.

'However, there was something . . . At what time was the road accident?'

'Soon after eleven; say just short of a quarter past.'

'And how long would you imagine it would take a man to get from here to the point at which the accident took place?'

'In the dark . . . Having to find gates . . . Twenty minutes, or maybe a bit more. But that's pure guesswork.'

'If we accept that figure, we're back to roughly five to eleven. And if my memory's correct, that's about the time when Nurse Trott, who was off duty and in her bedroom, caused a commotion by screaming.'

'Because she'd been attacked? But you said there was no incident that night?'

'She screamed because she had a nightmare which frightened her very badly.'

'Then I'm sorry, but I just don't see the relevance of this.'

'Mr Ridley, that is the explanation which Nurse Trott

gave. It was not given directly to me, which from her point of view is perhaps as well. It is my experience that while young children may wake up screaming because of nightmares, adults do not.'

'Then you think . . . ?'

'The circumstances were such that I was not called upon to decide what really happened.' She saw that he was about to speak. 'Nor do I wish to give my opinion now. There are rules which govern not only the working lives of our nurses, but also their off-duty lives. While I demand adherence to the former, I am, I hope, sufficiently realistic to realize that the latter are mostly out-of-date.' She smiled briefly. 'The world is a very different place from when they were drawn up. Yet as matron, it is my duty to see that while they exist, any official breach of them is dealt with.'

'You're saying . . .' He stopped, uncertain how to put the question tactfully.

'I'm saying that a blind eye is an advantage to people other than admirals.'

'Then it would be best if I had a word with Nurse Trott on my own?'

'Probably essential.' Again that quick smile.

'Can you tell me what kind of a person she is?'

'Intelligent, quick-witted, attractive, and something of an iconoclast, which at her age is right and proper.'

'Would you also say she's . . . well, sexy?'

'I feel you are better qualified to answer that than I.' She reached across to the intercom, but did not immediately press down on the switch on which her forefinger rested. 'I think I'll ask her to see you in the almoner's waiting-room. That can fairly be called neutral territory.'

The waiting-room was a lot more cheerful than he had expected. The walls were painted in two shades of green, there were four comfortable chairs and a settee, on the low, glass-topped table were a number of up-to-date magazines of general interest, and the four framed prints on the walls were of attractive, colourful country scenes.

Nurse Trott was an extremely attractive blonde with an artless manner which at one and the same time made a man both protective and hopeful. She was also very wary. She expressed surprise and excitement at meeting a real detective and even more surprise when it turned out that the detective was interested in the night she had screamed. She began to explain just how frightening that nightmare had been . . .

'You're sure it wasn't something else which made you scream?'

'Of course not.' She was very wide-eyed.

'The matron was saying that young kids wake up screaming from nightmares, but she'd never known an adult to do so.'

'She said that?'

'Yes.'

'Oh! . . . Well, she's wrong. I did.'

'You remember I'm investigating the hit-and-run case and one of my jobs is to trace out what the dead man was doing before the accident?'

'Of course I remember you telling me that. Which is why I don't see how I can possibly help.'

'By telling me if you screamed because you were threatened or attacked by a man?'

'If anything like that had happened, I'd have reported it.'

'Unless the circumstances were such that you didn't dare report them.'

'I don't know what you mean.'

'Miss Trott, the matron is quite a woman.'

'She can be an old battle-axe.'

'She probably has to be, with you lot to keep an eye on.' She giggled.

'She's convinced you were breaking the rules that night.'

'Of course I wasn't.'

'But she hasn't been called upon officially to decide whether you were so she's prepared to play at being Nelson.'

'To play at what?'

'To put the telescope to the blind eye.'

She nibbled at her lower lip.

'I'll lay it straight down the line. All I'm interested in is what really happened; how it affects anyone here doesn't concern me. And matron's not asking me to pass on to her what you say to me. But if you don't tell me what I've got to know, I'll have to start asking around and then things can't remain all nice and private and pretty soon matron's going to have to take official note of what's going on. And that means, no more blind eye.'

She looked at him for a while, then made up her mind. She spoke with great earnestness, conveying the fact that she was sharing her deepest secrets with him because she recognized a soul-mate. Everyone was agreed that the rules governing the conduct of nurses who lived in were positively Victorian—just imagine, no visitors allowed except in public rooms and all visitors to be off the premises by seven at night. It positively cramped a girl's style. Especially if the boyfriend hadn't anywhere to take her when they wanted to be alone. So it was accepted practice to smuggle a friend into the nurses' wing; dinner was the best time for getting him in because authority was busy eating, between two and five in the morning the safest time for him to leave. It was, of course, almost impossible to keep a visit secret from one's friends and neighbours, but it was absolutely essential to keep it from the sister in charge of the nurses' wing and the cleaning women. A week ago on Wednesday, she'd smuggled Bill in. Bill was . . . someone special. And this was the last quarter of the twentieth century and only the dodos believed that there was still one law for the man and another for the woman. And what harm did it do if it was a deep relationship, based on love . . .

'You were in bed together?'

She found that rather too direct and blushed.

The lucky bastard, he thought. 'So what happened to make you scream?'

She became even more embarrassed, rather upsetting the image of a daughter of liberation. It seemed that their love had blossomed, almost to the point of fruition, when she'd looked by chance at the window and had seen a truly horrific face staring at her . . . She'd screamed from shock—and, perhaps, also from a sense of outraged modesty. Whereupon, she'd found herself faced with the necessity of explaining what had frightened her, without disclosing Bill's presence . . .

'Where did he disappear to?' Ridley asked, more from curiosity than because it was of any importance.

'The cupboard. It's rather small and he was terribly uncomfortable.'

And, perhaps only temporarily, frustrated. 'You didn't tell anyone you'd seen this face?'

'I couldn't, could I?'

He wondered if she'd ever stopped to realize what the tragic consequences could have been of remaining silent. 'From what you've said, the curtains weren't drawn. Yet you and Bill . . .' Tactfully, he did not finish.

'I don't like being closed in and my bedroom's on the first floor so I never draw them. I didn't think anyone could ever look in.'

Nobody had told her about ladders. 'How would you describe this face?'

Her description was poor which, considering the circumstances, was not really to be wondered at, but it did convince him that the man's face had been concealed by some kind of a mask.

There was little more she could add and he thanked her for her help and promised her, on his honour as a gentleman, that he'd tell no one else at the hospital what she'd just told him.

He left the building and stood on the lawn outside the nurses' wing and worked out in which direction Ailsham cricket ground lay. Then he returned to the car, opened the boot, and changed into a pair of wellingtons. He walked across the park and went through a gateway, across a lane, and over a metal five-bar gate into a fifteen-acre field that was down to permanent pasture, but too sodden even to carry sheep. The man's route lay almost directly to the opposite corner. He searched the thorn hedge on either side for a distance of fifty feet, then crossed the field and searched there. There was a break in the hedge which had been stopped with a hurdle that now lay on its side. He went through, into another and larger field, down to winter wheat. He thought he could make out footprints which crossed the field. He went round the edge to a thin belt of trees beyond and near a clump of brambles he found a woollen ski mask. The pattern picked out eyes, nose, and mouth, in different colours from the background. He imagined what it must have been like to be making love and to look up suddenly to see that at the window and he wondered if the experience had left Nurse Trott with a neurosis.

On his return to the station, Ridley collected the OC file and carried this through to the DI's room. He read through the summary of cases from all over the country, stretching back over the past year, which had been reported and investigated without success, but not closed, for whatever reason. At the end of forty minutes, he had picked out three rapes, one attempted rape, and one sexual assault, each of which had been carried out by a man who had been described as having a face from a horror film.

CHAPTER 15

On Monday evening, a blustery, rain-threatening evening, Arnold was too preoccupied with his problems to realize what a strange figure he cut in the district. There was no mistaking his clerkiness, just as there was no mistaking the fact that in this part of Lewisham at times the writ of the law might not run very far. Several times in his walk from the bus stop he was eyed speculatively, but his very indifference to what lay about him provided a protection. He reached his destination and spoke to a slatternly woman who said that bloody Fred was down in the bloody pub where he was every bloody evening, spending the money she bloody needed.

The pub, on a corner site, was wedge-shaped. Dean was in the larger of the bars, drinking heavily. He was a small, foxy man who might have looked less untrustworthy if he had cut off his Zapata moustache. It really was astonishing that, two years before, the jury had found him not guilty.

'I can't say I do remember you,' said Dean uneasily.

'We met in court.'

'Never been in no court.'

'When Mr Vernay got you off that charge of housebreaking in Reading.'

'Yeah? . . . Well, maybe now I do remember a bit.'

'I'd like a little chat, if you've time?' He looked at the bar. 'What will you have?'

'If you're asking, it's a large brandy and ginger.'

Arnold bought the drinks and Dean suggested they went over to an empty table close to the outside door. They sat and Dean drank quickly, reckoning that if he had to cut and run for it, he might as well leave an empty glass behind.

'D'you remember what you said to Mr Vernay and me after the trial was over?'

'Can't say as I do.'

'That if ever you could do either of us a favour, we only needed to ask.'

'I said that?' Dean was astonished and disbelieving.

'I've come to ask you to do me a favour now.'

Dean's manner became very much more confident. 'There's favours and favours.' He fiddled with his glass to remind the other that it needed refilling.

Arnold, who hadn't yet touched his whisky, took the glass over to the bar. As the barmaid refilled it, he noticed how grubby her frock was. It completed the picture of slatternly failure and small-time villainy in which he found himself; he would have entered hell and supped with the Devil to help Elham.

He returned to the table. Dean drank, then said: 'So what's it all about?'

'I want you to do a job.'

'Jesus!' Dean was shocked by such stupidity. He looked round, but the table nearest to them was unoccupied and the couple at the one beyond were in a clinch and even the Last Trump might not have disturbed them. 'Are you round the twist, talking like that?' he demanded in a fierce whisper. 'And I don't have nothing to do with that sort of thing.' Then he realized that Arnold would have seen his list of previous convictions and he amended his denial. 'Leastwise, not since I got off when I hadn't done the job.'

'But you'd had plenty of experience before then?'

'That ain't nothing to do with you. I've done me bird. Look, mister, I'm finishing this drink and then I'm clearing off. And don't never come near me again.'

Arnold had not supposed that Dean would help him merely from a sense of gratitude. 'I'm willing to pay.'

'For what?'

'Carrying out a burglary.'

Dean was scared. Scared that this was all a trick, lining him up for the Norwich job which had gone badly wrong and left him only one small step ahead of the law. He hastily stood, picked up his glass and emptied it. 'You try and follow me and I'll do you rotten.' It was a ridiculous threat; he did not have the bearing of a man who would ever use physical violence.

Arnold produced an envelope. Certain it was hidden from everyone but Dean, he opened it and riffled through the corners of the twenty-pound notes. A man of simple tastes, he had for years saved a large proportion of his income and he had several thousand pounds in a building society account. He was prepared to spend everything.

Dean stared at the money and he started to think. The coppers wouldn't ever use someone in Arnold's position. And Arnold was dead serious. Only a right fool turned his back on easy money . . .

The Jaguar turned into the drive of Oak Tree Cottage and came to a smooth halt. Elham climbed out, switched on the torch, and went round the bonnet to open the front passenger door, but Penelope had forestalled him and was already standing on the drive.

'Don't forget,' she said.

'I won't.'

'Don't let him be all nauseatingly hypocritical.'

He wondered whether she still underestimated the strength of Rickmore's convictions or whether her words were merely a sign of how desperately nervous she was.

They walked towards the gate into the garden, buffeted by the gusty wind. The beam of the torch picked out a puddle. 'Mind that, dear.'

'Why can't he get the drive properly surfaced. It's like a slum.'

Had she ever allowed herself to understand what a slum was really like? Almost certainly not. She lived in a world where money put an impenetrable barrier between herself and slums. But if they failed tonight, that barrier would come crashing down . . . How to find the words that would convince Rickmore . . .

He opened the gate and they passed through. She complained about the unevenness of the brick path and said that if she didn't break an ankle, she'd be lucky. He liked this path, which wasn't really uneven, because it was so in character with the house. He'd always gone along with her desire for the new and the smart, but he knew a respect for the past which she lacked.

When they reached the small porch, he shone the torch on the bellpush, pressed it. They could look through the nearest hall window and they saw Rickmore step out of the sitting-room. He was wearing a polo-neck sweater and a pair of creased grey flannels. Elham imagined his wife's thoughts. Dressed like a tramp, as usual. He wondered, surprising himself by doing so, whether she'd ever dressed for comfort rather than effect? But perhaps she couldn't face the world without protection.

The porch light was switched on. When he identified them, Rickmore could not conceal his astonishment. He greeted them and now amazement had been replaced by reserve. Guessing the object of the visit, thought Elham, but not the content. They went inside.

'We hadn't seen you for such ages,' said Penelope in her most social voice, 'so I said we simply must pop in and find out how you both were. Aren't you going to kiss me hullo?' The ugliness of their last meeting might never have been.

Rickmore kissed her on the right cheek.

'Both, continental style.'

He kissed her on the left cheek.

'How's the new book coming along?'

'I'm afraid I've been neglecting it recently.'

She failed, or appeared to fail, to see any connection between recent times and the hit-and-run case. 'We went to a cocktail party the other evening and when I mentioned to our host that you were my brother-in-law, he was very much more impressed than when I told him Terence was taking Silk. So you see, you're famous.'

'And so a fool?'

'What do you mean?'

'"As yet a child, nor yet a fool to fame . . ."'

She was confused, yet determined not to appear to be. 'Sometimes, Dennis, you really do say the most amusing things.'

Anne came out of the sitting-room. 'I thought I recognized the voices.'

'It's such ages since we last saw you both.' Penelope came forward and embraced her sister, careless that there was no response; some of the jewels on her fingers sparkled as she moved under the overhead light.

'Come on in here where it's a sight warmer than in the hall,' said Anne, as soon as she had disengaged herself.

In the sitting-room, Penelope, who frequently complained of feeling cold, sat in the armchair nearer the fire. Elham hesitated, then said: 'D'you mind if I stand for a bit? Been sitting all day.' He took up his accustomed position with his back to the fire.

'What will you drink?' Rickmore asked. 'There's sherry, red Vermouth, or Scotch.'

Penelope chose Vermouth, Elham Scotch.

Conversation, while Rickmore moved around with glasses, was brittle; they were four people who were trying to ignore what had been said the last time they met, because that was the civilized way to behave, yet were unable actually to forget.

Elham drank quickly, put his glass down on an occasional

table. He coughed. 'We've just learned something very important.' He paused, but when there was no comment, he added: 'The police have identified the dead man.'

'Who was he?' asked Rickmore.

'His name was Tamworth. He had one conviction for indecent assault. Beyond that, the police are satisfied that he has been responsible for three rapes, one attempted rape, and one sexual assault, although he was not charged with any of these because of lack of evidence.'

There was a silence, broken only by a hiss as part of a log suddenly began to flame.

Elham leaned forward with his shoulders slightly hunched, an attitude he often adopted in court. 'You do realize what that means, don't you?'

'I don't know, not yet. It takes a bit of thinking about.'

'It's obvious,' said Penelope.

'Is it?'

She ignored the worried look her husband gave her. 'He was a filthy pervert. God knows how many women he molested.'

'Almost certainly many more than reported having been raped or assaulted,' said Elham.

'He deserved to die,' said Penelope viciously.

Rickmore said slowly: 'Deserved?'

'That's right.'

'I can't accept that.'

'Why? Because you're a typical man? You think there's no such thing as rape, it's always initially encouraged by the woman who then panics and tries to stop? But it's often not like that and it wasn't this time.' She turned. 'Just tell him, Terence.'

'I know the details of two of the cases,' said Elham. 'In each, the woman was grabbed as she was walking along a street at night, threatened with a knife to her throat, made to walk to somewhere dark where she was forced to strip and then subjected to the most obscene assaults.'

'How ghastly,' murmured Anne.

There was another silence. Penelope broke it. 'He deserved to die,' she said, even more pugnaciously than before.

Rickmore said: 'He obviously was a vile menace. But when you say "deserved to die", where's your authority?' As always, when he became excited or earnest, his slight speech impediment became more noticeable.

Anne, worried by the impression her husband was now giving, said: 'Dennis, all Penny is saying is that that kind of a man is so great a menace that he's better dead than alive. Surely not even you can argue against that?'

'I can start by asking, better from whose point of view?'

'For goodness sake!' snapped Penelope. 'From the point of view of all the women he'd have raped if he'd gone on living. Or are you now so liberal that you think they don't matter at all?'

'It's not a case of being liberal, or anything like that, it's not setting myself up as God. I don't know what motivated him. Suppose he was subjected to overwhelming desires, so overwhelming that he was totally unable to resist them; that morality and self-will simply had no meaning for him?'

'You've not begun to understand. He's better dead because now he can't rape any more women.'

Rickmore spoke quietly to Elham. 'You did say he had one conviction, but in all the other cases there was not enough evidence to charge him?'

'That's right.'

'Then he may well have had nothing to do with them?'

'The police are satisfied he did.'

'Maybe. But thankfully we live in a country where police certainty isn't enough to convict. I repeat, he may not have comitted any of those other offences. In which case, all he'd ever been guilty of was one indecent assault. A man can commit one such act, be caught, and be so shocked by his conviction that he never does such a thing again. Then surely no one can say he deserves to die?'

'Dennis,' said Anne angrily, 'you're being very stupid.'

'Because I refuse to give way to emotion?'

'Because you're arguing just for the sake of arguing.'

'That's unfair and untrue.'

'Dennis,' said Elham, 'the police aren't as blindly biased as you obviously think. They've traced out Tamworth's movements on the night he died. He went to Hacksley House, the geriatric hospital, and used a ladder to get up to one of the nurses' rooms. She saw a hideous face at the window and screamed, which alarmed Tamworth, who fled. In a copse half way between the hospital and the cricket ground, they found a ski-mask, which the nurse identified as having been worn by the man at the window; it also fits the description given by two of the women previously assaulted. His build matches the description of one woman's assailant and she stated that the fingers of the man were noticeably short and stubby and the nails looked disgusting because they were constantly being bitten and so had retreated part of the way down the fingers—Tamworth's fingers were very short and stubby and his nails had retreated from constant biting . . . There can be no reasonable doubt that he was guilty of several sexual assaults.'

'Then I'll accept that he was.'

'You're satisfied?' demanded Penelope.

'Satisfied that he was probably a rapist, yes; I've just said so.'

'And if he hadn't died, he'd have continued to commit rape and sexual assaults?' asked Elham.

'I suppose that has to follow.'

'Then he was better off dead,' snapped Penelope.

Rickmore's expression hardened, but he said nothing.

Elham picked up his glass and drained it, replaced the

glass on the table. 'You'll have realized why I've told you this?'

'I imagine so.'

'Without renewing the argument about whether he deserved to die, it's clear that by his death an unknown number of women are saved the most revolting of experiences. Those women would certainly regard his death as an act of providence.'

'That's taking things too far . . .'

'It is not,' cut in Anne fiercely.

Rickmore looked at her. He had lost all her understanding and sympathy.

'I wasn't negligent in hitting him,' said Elham. 'He ran straight out into the path of the car because he was panicking, fearing pursuers were immediately behind him. I had absolutely no chance of avoiding him. It is true that I did not stop. If I had, I'd have been breathalysed and probably would have been found to be over the limit. In those circumstances, it's inevitable that it would have been held that the accident was to a large extent due to my intoxication and there would have been nothing I could have said that would have refuted that presumption. Yet it would have been totally wrong. I could not have missed hitting him if I had not had a drop of liquor for the previous week.

'You said I should have stopped; that it could have been a situation where his life depended on how soon aid could be summoned. But the alarm was given by the other driver very soon after I could have given it, so very little time was lost. In fact, time was not of the essence. Nothing would have changed for Tamworth if I had stopped.

'You have told the police certain facts which identify me as the driver. If you confirm that evidence, I'll be charged, probably with causing death by reckless driving, and will be found guilty. I will be imprisoned or given a suspended sentence. My career will be finished and my life ruined. Can you now, in the light of what I've told you, bear that responsibility?'

'You're claiming . . .'

'I am claiming nothing. I am asking you to understand that the law does not always serve justice; to recognize that in some cases the law can be as merciless as the criminal.'

'And you're also putting forward the proposition that a crime can be excused if the victim deserved to be the victim. That can't possibly be right. Crime is crime and the nature of the victim is irrelevant.'

'Are you still going to tell the police?' demanded Penelope shrilly.

'I . . . I don't know.'

'You swine!'

'Penny . . .' began Elham.

'Haven't you the courage to say it to his face? Well, I have. All he wants to do is to see you in prison and me reduced to rags. He's always been so jealous of us that he couldn't even be polite.'

'I am not, and never have been, jealous of either of you,' Rickmore said angrily. 'And if you won't believe me, ask Anne.'

Anne looked away, unable to confirm his words.

They were in their bedroom, but had not yet begun to undress. 'Why won't you understand?' demanded Rickmore.

'Because I can't begin to see how you can believe it's more important to honour the law than to help Penny and Terence.'

'You've got to forget what kind of a man Tamworth was.'

'Forget? How can I forget? For God's sake, climb down from that ivory perch. Penny was absolutely right. He deserved to die. And if I'd been driving, I'd feel I'd served justice, not betrayed it. And don't start talking about principles. Just tell me why it's so important to ruin your own relations.'

'You really do think it's jealousy?'

'I . . . I just don't know what to think. I can't understand how you can go on and on and on as you are.'

'Because the law is our only defence against anarchy and if we betray it . . .'

'For Christ's sake, stop pontificating; just think on this. If that man hadn't been killed, I could have been his next victim. So what would you have felt about your wonderful justice if you'd come home to find me raped?'

He knew what he would have felt.

CHAPTER 16

Because it was impossible to live for long at a high level of emotional conflict, it was implicitly agreed that the subject should be dropped until Rickmore wanted to return to it. And because he'd been forced to accept that there was no way of escaping both Scylla and Charybdis—he would either have to betray his principles or destroy Elham's happiness and career in circumstances which appeared to make a mockery of his principles—throughout Tuesday he was careful never to broach the subject, even obliquely. But from time to time he'd seen Anne look at him with quick puzzlement and he'd known that she was trying to understand how he could find the decision so difficult a one to make.

On Wednesday morning, he went downstairs to the kitchen where she was cooking breakfast and he made an attempt to break the feeling of restraint between them. 'Eggs and bacon? What about our cholesterol levels?'

She responded to his lighter mood. 'Worry about yours,

not mine. I'm sticking to one piece of toast and an apple. But I decided you were beginning to look pinched around the face and it was time to fill you up a bit. And since we normally have so little fried food, I can't believe this one indulgence will clog your arteries.'

'You know the trouble with one indulgence? It breeds a second.'

'Try using some will-power.'

'In the olfactory face of eggs and bacon?'

'Instead of talking nonsense, see if the coffee's made. It should be, but I haven't heard the machine belch yet.'

He lifted the aluminium lid and coffee, which had been surging up the central spout, splattered him. 'There's a law which states that one always checks at the most dangerous moment.'

'Did it reach your coat?'

'No, only the back of my hand.'

'That's all right, then.'

'Even if I'm severely burned?'

'If you'd been even lightly burned, you'd now be shouting for an ambulance.' She turned away from the stove and kissed him lightly. Then she turned back and used the bottom of the slice to surge hot fat over the yolks of the two eggs. 'I've buttered a piece of toast and it's on the plate— push it over, will you?'

He passed it to her and she began to dish. 'You've got a clean handkerchief to go to work with, haven't you?'

'No.'

She placed the two rashers of bacon to the side of the toast, lifted up the eggs and placed them on the toast. She handed him the plate. 'Go and eat. You're a bit behind time.'

'Not to worry, my hours are flexible.'

'Do Teerson Products know that?'

He carried the plate through to the dining-room and sat

at the table. She appeared in the doorway. 'Did you say a moment ago you did have a clean handkerchief?'

'I said I didn't.'

'That's odd.'

'Why?' But she'd returned into the kitchen and didn't answer him. He cut the yolks of the eggs and let them run over the toast, then started eating.

She came into the dining-room, a mug of coffee in each hand. She passed him one, put one in front of her place setting, then returned to the kitchen for a tray on which were toast, butter, an apple, and a jar of marmalade. She began to quarter and peel the apple.

'You didn't say what was odd about the clean handkerchief I haven't got?' he said.

She ate a piece of apple. 'You know yesterday you needed one for work and there weren't any respectable ones in your cupboard? I knew there was one of the new ones in the load of laundry I'd put on the ironing-board.' She ate another piece of apple. 'But when I went into the spare room this morning, I couldn't find it, so I naturally thought you must have taken it . . . Are you sure you didn't?'

'Quite sure.'

'Then where on earth's it got to?'

'Search me. And I hasten to add that that won't solve the puzzle.'

'Then where is it?'

'A good question.'

'But no answer?'

'Not this early in the morning . . . By the way, the bacon's rather salty.'

'Is it? I'm sorry. I bought it in one of the supermarkets in Reckton and their bacon's never as good as the stuff the local shop sells, but it's a lot cheaper.'

'Champagne tastes, beer income, that's me.'

'Who's any different? . . . And come to that, now I think

about it, the pile of washing was different.'

'Being of a fairly logical mind, I fail to follow you. Or to put it another way, I don't know what the hell you're talking about.'

'I've a funny habit which probably means I'm suffering from some deep and quite unmentionable repression that whenever I move a pile of freshly laundered clothes, I always make certain I put it down exactly square to whatever I put it on. Yesterday I unwrapped the parcel—we had to have the washing done at the laundry because our machine was on the blink—and I put the pile down on the ironing-board, meaning to take it upstairs later, but I forgot. This morning, it was slightly caterwise to the board. Did you move it?'

'Why should I?'

'Looking for a clean handkerchief.'

'Remember something? I haven't got one.'

'Yes, I know . . .'

He ate the last piece of egg and toast, put the plate on one side. 'Shove the toast over, will you?' Then he noticed her expression. 'Is something wrong?'

'I . . . I'm not certain. I suppose really I'm being very silly'

'That sounds unlikely.'

'The thing is, I'm wondering if something funny has been going on.'

'In what way?'

'The handkerchief missing, the pile of washing that's been moved, and . . . Dennis, I woke up in the middle of the night and there just didn't seem to be any reason why. And then I thought I heard a noise in the kitchen.'

'What kind of a noise?'

'I don't know, really. A kind of clink, as if something had touched something else.'

'A mouse charging around in clogs?'

'When I didn't hear anything more, I decided it must

have been a mouse—without the clogs. But now . . . You don't think we had someone in the house last night, do you?'

He was startled by the suggestion. 'Presumably the front door was locked when you came down this morning?'

'Yes. And when I opened up, everything was as it should be.'

'Then it had to be a mouse you heard, or the house turning over in its sleep; and for once you did not line up the washing with geometric certainty on the ironing-board, and my one new clean handkerchief has been lost at the laundry and I'll have to go on using an old one with holes in it. People will say my wife neglects me.'

'And you'll agree?'

'Enthusiastically.'

Looking now at Reginald Gilles—pronounced Gil-lays—it was difficult to imagine his winning the 220 yards and quarter-mile for his college because the years had crinkled his flesh and his wife's death had seared his mind. But that did not mean that he was ready to accept the loss of many of his sporting trophies with equanimity.

'The damned scoundrel's taken all the best ones,' he said furiously.

The detective-constable decided he looked exactly like an old bantam cock.

'They're irreplaceable.'

The DC stared at the glass-fronted showcase.

'You've got to get them back for me.'

'We'll do our best.' By now, they had probably been hammered flat and melted down.

'How could anyone stoop to taking something so obviously personal?'

Poor old bastard, thought the DC; never come to terms with the modern world. Perhaps he thought that villains still had scruples.

'And what's more, the damned man helped himself to a drink!'

The DC had to work hard not to smile at that. But he'd been told to treat the old boy with respect. He'd been chairman of the magistrates for a number of years and could almost certainly still raise a stink if he felt the police were treating him with indifference or condescension. 'As far as you know, sir, is anything more missing?'

'I haven't checked. When I came in here and saw me trophies had gone . . .' He stopped abruptly. It was difficult to explain, but a little more of his life had just been taken from him.

'Do you have a safe?'

'Yes, but there's not much in it. Gave all my wife's jewellery to my daughter-in-law. But I don't think she really likes any of it. Bit old-fashioned, I suppose, but it's been in the family for quite a time. As I said to my son, if Erica doesn't want to wear it, keep it and pass it on to your daughter. It's comforting to see something go down the generations.'

It was comforting to have some jewellery for oneself, never mind the next generation; they could look after themselves. The old boy must have been well-heeled. Probably still was, only one wouldn't think so, looking at the way he dressed and the state of repair and decoration of the house. 'Would you check now and see if the safe was forced? And then make certain nothing else is missing?'

'The cups and medals are insured, of course, but it's the sentimental value that matters.'

You keep the sentiment, I'll take the insurance payout, the DC thought as Gilles walked out of the room, his leg movements laboured from arthritis. The DC went over to the nearest of the three windows. One pane had been smashed and then the intruder had reached in and unlatched the window. A crude method of entry into a house in which only one man, hard of hearing, lived. A draught of cold, damp air came through the broken window as he looked out. Stretching away from the outside wall was a flowerbed in need of weeding, and he saw a clear footprint in the soft earth. Chummy was not only crude, but careless. He moved out of the draught and visually examined the room. Furniture had a look of class about it, but the upholstery was faded and in places tattered; the huge carpet must have cost a bomb when it was new, but that was a long time ago; pictures, with display lights, for which he wouldn't have bid a quid, but which might well be worth a lot more than he'd ever see; a carved wooden overmantel which incorporated a mirror that reflected the central chandelier—shades of high life; a mobile cocktail cabinet with a split top that opened out to form two shelves at the same time as a shelf of bottles and glasses rose up to that level . . . He went over and examined it. On the right-hand leaf was a bottle of Haig and a glass. Gilles had said that he hadn't used that glass, so Chummy had. There might just be prints on it; there were still one or two villains who were so thick they didn't know about fingerprints. And if Gilles had to be bullshitted into believing his peasant-sized robbery was receiving the full attention of the police, taking the glass for testing would be a good move . . .

He returned to the show cabinet. The ornamental key had been in the lock, so there'd been no problem about opening the door. Because of the key's design, there'd not be any decipherable prints on it . . .

Gilles returned. 'Found the safe, but he didn't open it.'

'Would you show me where it is, sir?'

They went along one corridor, wood-panelled and dark, turned into another that was even darker, and then almost immediately entered a small room furnished with only a table, a chair, and two paintings. One of the paintings was on hinges and it had been swung back to reveal a safe.

The safe's make was Mackay and the DC knew that the firm had ceased production fifty years or more before; even then, they'd been known more for their fire-resistant qualities than their security. A clever twirler would have cracked it in one minute flat. That it hadn't been forced confirmed that the intruder was useless. Some young punk on hard drugs who needed to buy his next fix and didn't care what risks he took. 'I'll have that checked for dabs, sir, so maybe you'll leave opening it until I say?'

'Of course.'

'Have you any valuables anywhere else in the house that need checking?'

'I don't think so. My wife and I gave my son a great many things when he married. It seemed to us that that was the sensible thing to do, because when one gets old . . .'

The DC blocked. He didn't want to know about old age.

They returned to the drawing-room and the DC had one last look round, and this was when he found the candy-striped handkerchief on the floor behind the sofa. He picked it up. 'Is this yours, sir?'

'No. I never use anything but white.'

The handkerchief had been recently laundered and there was a mark on one corner. It began to look as if Chummy was not only crude and careless, but stupid as well.

CHAPTER 17

Macey, specialists in dry-cleaning delicate fabrics as well as general cleaners, was owned and run by a husband and wife. The wife, a small bustling woman, seldom quite still, said to the CID aide: 'Let's see the handkerchief and I'll tell you.'

He produced a plastic bag, extracted a candy-striped handkerchief, and handed it over.

She examined it very briefly. 'Yes, that's our mark.'

'Can you say who it belongs to?'

'Certainly, once I've checked the records.'

She turned round and opened the middle drawer of a metal filing cabinet, flicked through the cards inside, then came to a stop. 'The name's Mrs Rickmore.'

'How d'you spell that?'

She told him.

'Are there any initials?'

'D.P.'

'What about an address?'

'I haven't one. We don't deliver any more, so there's no call for them.'

He read through what he'd written a second time. He'd been working with CID for only two weeks and was still obsessively conscientious.

Ridley, sitting behind the desk in the DI's room, said: 'Did you say Rickmore?'

'That's right, skipper,' said the CID aide.

That was quite a coincidence. 'D'you get any initials or an address?'

'Initials are D.P. The laundry didn't have an address.'

'I just wonder . . . Right, that's it for the moment. You can get back on to the Swift job.'

The aide left. Ridley searched in the desk for a local telephone directory, found it, and checked the initials of the Rickmore who lived in Oak Tree Cottage, Yew Cross. D.P. So how in the hell had Rickmore's handkerchief appeared in a house that had been burgled?

Lineport, twelve miles from Reckton, had had a flourishing fishing trade until, starting some thirty years previously, spiralling costs had rendered the small inshore boats un-economic. There had never been any quays or docks; the fishing-boats had been winched up the gently sloping pebble beach, their keels protected by a wide metal band known as the Lineport guard. Now, the winch had rusted into immobility and few people remembered what the Lineport guard was.

The town had narrow, twisting streets and a population older than the national average; doctors were reluctant to practise there because so much of the work was geriatric. Sensibly, successive councils had tried to retain the atmos-phere and there had been very little development. The largest of the four antique shops was in a Georgian house which had once been owned by a wealthy man who'd seduced his maid and then murdered her when it appeared she was pregnant. He had been tried, found guilty, and hanged. The antique shop specialized in silver, but it also sold miniature scaffolds that were made from the wood of the original scaffold and these had always proved to be very popular. Luckily, despite the large numbers which had been sold over the years, there still seemed to be no lack of the original wood from which to make them.

On Saturday, a man entered and offered to sell a large and handsome silver-gilt cup. The owner of the shop exam-ined this and then asked what had happened to the plinth? The question disturbed the man, who muttered something to the effect that he didn't know whether he did want to sell the cup after all. He returned it to the holdall and hurried out.

The owner called his wife down into the shop and asked her to look after things while he went along to the police. He walked the short distance to the station and spoke to the detective-sergeant.

'Hullo, Mr Chapman, not seen you for quite a time. How are things—going all right? . . . Let's sit down over there

and then you can say what's up.' The DS led the way over
to a table and chairs. They sat.

Chapman was a precise man, inclined to speak pedanti-
cally. 'A little earlier, immediately before I came here, in
fact, a man came into my emporium and asked if I was
interested in buying a silver-gilt cup. It would be very
difficult to explain precisely why, but from the beginning I
was rather suspicious of his *bona fides*.'

'You've got a nose for these things, haven't you?'

'It's certainly big enough!' Chapman might be pedantic,
but he had a sense of humour. 'The cup had been set on a
plinth, but he did not produce this. When I asked him where
it was, he became nervous, said he was not certain after all
if he did wish to sell the cup, took it back, and left.'

'Went out in a hurry?'

'That is how I would describe his mode of departure.'

'What kind of a bloke was he?'

'He had a moustache, which I must say struck me as
looking false, but I'm wondering now whether that impression was perhaps due to my original suspicions. Other-
wise he was ordinary, neither short nor tall, with the kind
of face which is sometimes said, I believe, to melt into a
crowd. Much of his face was obscured by a cap with a large
peak.'

'Anything else at all about him that struck you?'

'Yes, there was. He had a very slight speech defect. Once
or twice he had trouble in pronouncing his R's.'

'How about this cup he tried to sell you—can you describe
it?'

'It was about eight inches tall, six in diameter, and shaped
in the style which is known in the trade—erroneously, in
my view—as Portland. It was silver-gilt, hallmarked in
London in nineteen twenty-one. It bore an inscription,
"Two hundred and twenty yards".'

The DS looked down at his notes. 'Your description's got

me wondering . . . Hang on, I shan't be long.' He left and was gone for a little over two minutes. When he returned, he had a sheet of paper in his hand. 'There was a robbery last Wednesday and a load of sporting trophies was pinched. The owner's given a list and this is it—as a matter of fact, you'd have had a copy before the day's out. What d'you think?' He passed the paper across.

Chapman read carefully and slowly, then looked up. 'It is very probable that the item listed as number six is the cup I was shown.'

'I thought it might be. And since there was a whole load of tiny shields listing winners' names, including Mr Gilles's three times, on the plinth, it would explain why you weren't offered that as well . . . I think we'll need a stronger description of this man.'

'I'm afraid I'm not very good at that sort of thing.'

'You're not doing yourself justice. Look how much you've given me already!' The DS was very good at persuading witnesses to tell far more than they'd realized they'd known.

Ridley put the receiver down. He leaned back in the chair and, with unfocused gaze, stared at the window. There was little doubt that the cup which had been offered for sale to Chapman in Lineport was one of those which had been stolen from Gilles. (All doubt would soon be resolved; Gilles had a photograph of himself receiving that cup and this photograph was going to be shown to Chapman.) At Gilles's house, a handkerchief belonging to D. P. Rickmore had been found. The aide who'd taken the handkerchief to be identified had forgotten to ask the cleaners whether they had more than one D. P. Rickmore on their books, but it was a small omission, soon put right—and what were the odds against? Chapman's description of the man who'd come into the antique shop had not been good generally;

specifically, however, it had been promising. The man spoke with a very slight speech impediment.

Ridley picked up a pencil and fiddled with it. The investigating DC had pointed out that the burglary had been carried out by someone with little skill or experience. To offer that silver cup for sale only a dozen miles from where it had been stolen suggested either stupidity or no knowledge whatsoever of how the police worked. Rickmore spoke with a slight speech defect . . . But it strained credulity to imagine that he would suddenly take up burglary unless so desperately strapped financially that he was faced by disaster. Although he obviously wasn't wealthy, equally, he showed no signs of poverty . . . There was something here which Ridley couldn't grasp, perhaps because the conclusion to which the facts pointed was contrary to common sense. For the first time since he'd moved into the DI's room, he felt unequal to the job and wished there were someone he could go to for advice and instruction. He swore. It was not a feeling he liked.

Rickmore finished washing down the Escort and squeezed out the leather. Considering the mileage the car had done, it was a reasonable runner, but only an optimist could think it had many more miles left to go. Was he the only PRO in the country who did not have a company car? What was it like to be so well off that one could walk into a showroom and order the car of one's choice? What was life like when money—or rather, the lack of it—ceased to be central to everything one did or considered doing? Which brought him back to Elham.

He picked up the bucket, carried it across to the spile fence, and threw the dirty water into the small orchard which lay between the road and the garden. He left the bucket and leather to dry in the near corner of the garage.

He walked round the house and entered the porch where

he changed out of wellingtons into shoes. Anne was in the kitchen, cooking. 'Are you doing anything?' she asked.

'I have been and I'm about to.'

'Good. Will you chop an onion up for me? They make me cry so.'

'Why not use those goggles you were given?'

'They steam up.'

'Be difficult!'

'You know they hardly ever affect you.'

'If I have tears, prepare to shed them now.' He picked an onion out of the vegetable rack, carried it across to a working surface, reached across for the board she'd been using, and brought down a steel knife from the magnetized strip. 'I've been thinking.' He sliced off the two ends, began to peel away the skin. 'About Terence.'

'Oh!' She looked at him, then quickly away. It was the first time the subject had been broached since the night Elham had told them that the dead man had been identified.

'I can't do it.'

'What can't you do?' she asked tightly.

'Be directly responsible for ruining him, the circumstances being what they are.'

'Thank God for that.'

He finished peeling the onion, cut it longitudinally several times. 'I couldn't face the knowledge that I'd wrecked his whole life. I'm right in principle—but I've learned something you knew from the beginning. Principles can be right, but the observing of them wrong.' He cut the onion at right angles to the previous cuts.

'When are you going to tell him?'

'I'll phone . . .'

'No. It's something you've got to do face to face.'

'I was afraid you'd say that.'

'Will it help if I come and hold your hand?'

'Squeeze it hard.'

'To try to stop you thinking?'

'You know me too well for my own comfort.'

She carried the casserole dish with the mince in it over to where he stood and used a wooden spoon to sweep the diced onion on to the mince. Then she kissed him. 'And love what I know.'

The suggestion didn't come from either of them, and it was without a word being spoken that Anne and Rickmore left the parked car and walked round to the front door of Popham House, instead of the back.

Penelope opened the door and her astonishment was complete. She stared at them, the surprise slowly giving way to tension.

'May we come in?' asked Anne.

She moved to one side and they entered.

'Is Terence in?'

She nodded.

Rickmore said: 'I want to tell him something.'

They went through to the blue sitting-room. Elham had identified their voices and he now stood, not in front of the fire, but by the armchair in which he invariably sat. On the table by his side was a cut-glass tumbler half filled with whisky and soda.

'Dennis wants to talk to you,' said Penelope unnecessarily.

'Well?' Elham tried to give the impression of defiance; an impression denied by his expression.

Rickmore said: 'I'm going to tell the police that after all I can't be certain about the state of the car or the garage.'

Elham reached for the glass and picked it up with a hand that shook. Penelope began to cry silently, tears welling out of her eyes and coursing down her cheeks.

CHAPTER 18

Ridley braked the CID Metro to a halt, switched off the engine, and climbed out. The wind had freshened and he zipped up the front of his parka before crossing the pavement and opening the front gate of No. 64.

The front garden, even at this time of the year, was tidy. MacMahon, he recalled, was a keen gardener who spent much of his spare time cutting this, planting that, digging here, weeding there. Since he lived in a police house and when he retired would have to leave it, Ridley considered all that work a stupid waste of time and effort. But then, it was totally short-sighted to live in a police house and these days a policeman with any sense invested in a place of his own. But in every respect, MacMahon was of the old school.

Ridley rang the front-door bell and Mrs MacMahon opened the door. She was a large, rather coarsely featured woman who had never been physically very attractive, even when young, but who was possessed of an unmistakably warm nature. 'Hullo, Steve.'

''Morning, Mrs MacMahon. Sorry to bother you like this on a Sunday, but I was wondering if it would be all right to have a bit of a chat with the boss?'

'According to the doctor you shouldn't, that's for sure, not if it's business. But I reckon it'll do more good than harm. A bear with a sore head would be better company than he's been since he got back from hospital. Never could stand being idle.'

'How is he?'

'He seems a lot better, but it's going to be a bit more time before we're certain. Seems they still can't tell whether he did have a slight heart attack and they've got to make more tests. Beats me—I thought you'd either had had one or you hadn't . . . But come on in, instead of standing out there in the cold.'

He stepped into the hall.

'He's in the front room. Tell him I'm making you some coffee and warming a cup of milk for him—and whatever he says, he's not getting coffee.'

He went into the sitting-room. MacMahon was on the settee, his legs up. 'Saw it was you through the window. How are things?'

'Not too bad. But more to the point, how are you?'

'Bloody fed up and bored. There's nothing wrong with me and the doctors are a bunch of old women . . . I expect Elsie's already told you that I'm impossible to live with?'

Ridley grinned.

'Sit down; there's no extra charge for a chair.'

He sat on a large, well-upholstered armchair which showed signs of wear. The MacMahons preferred comfort to style. 'The missus said to tell you that she's making me coffee and warming you up a cup of milk.'

MacMahon swore, but without much conviction.

Ridley said, with uncharacteristic diffidence: 'I've come looking for a bit of advice.'

'Let's hear the problem.'

'Old Gilles's place was done on Wednesday night.'

'Reginald Gilles, the man who used to do a lot of running and was chairman of the local bench for God knows how many years?'

'That's the bloke.'

MacMahon chuckled. 'I'll bet he had something to say about things.'

'He did! . . . It was only a small job and really only warranted someone from the uniform branch, but seeing it was him, I sent Alan.'

'Good thinking.'

'Alan says Chummy was a real beginner—stepped on to a flowerbed and left a good print, smashed a window to get in, nicked a load of silver cups that can't be worth all that much, but left a safe with quite a bit of cash in it. The safe was a Mackay and I reckon I could do it with a screwdriver. He helped himself to a drink and dropped a handkerchief with a laundry mark on it.

'Come yesterday, he—or a mate—was in one of the antique shops in Lineport trying to sell a large silver-gilt cup, missing its plinth, and with "Two hundred and twenty yards" engraved on it. Chapman, the owner, was suspicious and the man cleared off. The cup did come from Gilles's place.'

'Was Chapman able to give a reasonable description?'

'Not really. Could have been anyone, wearing a false moustache and a cap. But he did pick out one useful fact. The bloke had a slight speech defect and occasionally couldn't pronounce his R's properly.'

MacMahon saw that Ridley was looking at him intently, as if expecting some reaction. 'That's not much use on its own, is it?' he asked, worried that perhaps his brain wasn't working as quickly and clearly as it should.

'Suppose I add that we've identified the laundry mark and it's D. P. Rickmore's?'

'God's teeth!' exclaimed MacMahon, who sometimes used such ancient expletives when his surprise was too great for mere four-letter words.

'It all fits,' said Ridley exasperatedly, 'but who the bloody hell's ever going to believe that a bloke like Rickmore has suddenly taken up breaking and entering?'

'He could need money desperately?'

'Could he? He's not rolling in it, sure, but who is, except for a few lucky bastards? We both saw his place. He's not getting ready to queue at the soup kitchen.'

'No, he isn't.'

'Then who's going to believe it was him?'

'That depends on how strong the evidence becomes. If you know Chummy had a drink, presumably a glass was left around?'

'Glass and bottle. I've sent 'em both off for dabs.'

'What about comparison dabs from Rickmore?'

'One of the things I want to know is, do you think I should go for them yet?'

MacMahon thought for a moment. 'Probably not; at least, not openly. This has to be treated very, very carefully. After all, we wouldn't want . . .' He came to a sudden stop.

'What?'

There was no answer.

Ridley waited. MacMahon had the habit of disappearing into a brown study, which could be infuriating; but he'd come here to learn if any such brown study could bear fruit.

The door opened and Mrs MacMahon, carrying a tray, entered. Ridley stood and took the tray from her. 'Thanks, Steve. Just wait a moment while I clear a table.' She briefly studied her husband, worried that it might after all have been a mistake to allow Ridley to discuss work with him, but judged from his expression that it had not. She removed some newspapers from a small table. 'Put the tray down here and help yourself. There's milk and sugar and some biscuits.'

'Can I do your cup?'

'Will you? A little milk, but no sugar, thanks.'

'And what about me?' demanded MacMahon.

'No sugar and a whole cupful of milk,' she answered.

'That muck's only fit for calves and babies.'

She laughed and said that she'd rather look after a crèche full of babies than him.

Some fifteen minutes later she collected up the dirty cups, saucers and plates, put them on the tray, and left.

'What wouldn't I give for a double Scotch,' said Mac-Mahon longingly.

'Have you been knocked off that as well?' asked Ridley.

'Been knocked off everything that makes life worth living . . . Look, Steve, let's discuss motive. There's always a motive, except when you're dealing with freaks like psychopaths. Was the motive here financial?'

'What else?'

'You don't think it might have been to create a lever?'

'I don't get it,' said Ridley bluntly.

'Remember the circumstances. Elham, too much alcohol aboard to risk a breath test, runs away after the accident. Unexpectedly, Rickmore turns up at Popham House, sees the damage to the Jaguar and notices that the garage isn't damaged.

'We interview Rickmore and he gives evidence which provides a peg on which all the circumstantial evidence can be hung and which will nail Elham. Elham's a very smart lawyer who can appreciate the value in court of evidence better than we can. He sees clearly that if Rickmore can't be persuaded to change his evidence, he—that is, Elham—is for the chopper. So Rickmore's value as a witness for the prosecution has to be undermined to the point where no jury will believe him. What quicker way of doing that than making him appear to be a criminal?'

'Elham wouldn't do anything like that.'

'Why not? Because of his position? But it's precisely because of his position that he would. Think of all he stands to lose if he's found guilty of a serious crime.'

'But . . .'

'You're the one who's always sneering at the rich; are you sure you aren't now investing him with a sense of justice, honour, and fair-mindedness just because he *is* rich? He was willing to knock a man down and not stop, wasn't he?'

'That's different.'

'Is it?'

To his angry embarrassment, Ridley realized that Mac-Mahon was right—he had been instinctively supposing Elham incapable of deliberately entrapping another person in order to save himself.

'If you're thinking it could be different because they're related by marriage, just ask yourself, when did that ever stop two people disliking each other? Rickmore's never held back on the evidence. On the contrary, he volunteered the news of his drive over to Popham House without any prompting from us and we'd not have learned about it but for him. He's obviously no fool, so we must assume he realized the significance of what he was saying. He's not starving, but financially he's not in the same league as Elham. It can get on a man's wick to have a brother-in-law who goes out of his way to show how much better off he is. He may well have shown his jealousy, which will have exacerbated the ill-feeling between them. And can you imagine Elham's thoughts when he learned that it was Rickmore who'd fingered him? My guess is, he'd laugh all the way to the nearest bottle of champagne if Rickmore's nailed for something he didn't do.'

'I still can't see Elham setting it up. He hasn't enough balls.'

'Suppose you stood to lose everything you have and are faced with a future of poverty instead of luxury . . . Wouldn't your balls grow?'

'Maybe.'

'And remember one thing more. We first homed in on Elham through a tip-off. Who was the anonymous caller?'

'All we know is, a woman.'

'Prompted by Rickmore? Do you imagine that Elham hasn't worked that out?'

'You've got one hell of a mind! You've turned them into a couple of right royal bastards.'

'If I've learned one thing in the Force, it's that everyone can be a right royal bastard, given tight enough circumstances.'

'They're going to find that . . .'

'Steve, I said at the beginning that this was a case to be taken carefully. I'm telling you now, it's a powder keg. Whatever you do, remember Agag.'

'Where's he come into it?'

MacMahon smiled briefly.

'Are you going to ring now?' asked Anne.

Rickmore looked across at her. 'I wasn't, no.'

'You can't put it off for ever.'

'Not when you're around.' He stood, put a log on the fire.

'Get it over and done with. And remember, it's the right thing to do.'

'Is it?'

'You're not thinking of going back on what you said?'

'No. I'm just trying to convince myself that there really are times when circumstances change wrong into right.'

'Yes, there are.'

'Ever the pragmatist?'

'It makes life more liveable.'

He crossed the carpet and kissed her.

'You're lucky you married me, Dennis Rickmore.'

'You're always claiming that. Don't you think it would be more becoming to leave me to say it?'

'Haven't you realized yet that in the wrong hands you'd have developed into an impossible prig?'

'Thanks very much.'

'But as it is . . .'

'Finish and put me out of my agony.'

'You're one of the nicest men in the world.'

'I can resist everything except praise.' He kissed her a second time.

'Then what about temptation?'

'Let's find out.'

She smiled. 'Go and make the phone call and stop trying to lead me astray.'

He went into the hall and across to the telephone. This was his Rubicon; the moment when he betrayed his principles. Quickly, as if delay might make him renege, he checked the number and then dialled it, asked to speak to Detective-Inspector MacMahon.

'I'm afraid he's away ill.'

'I'm sorry to hear that,' he said automatically. 'Is Detective-Sergeant Ridley around?'

'I'll put you through to CID.'

'Duty DC speaking. Can I help you?'

'Will you give a message to Mr Ridley, please? My name's Rickmore. Will you say that I'm afraid I've realized I've made a mistake and my evidence regarding the damage to the Jaguar and the garage is wrong.'

The DC repeated the message.

Rickmore returned to the sitting-room.

'That was very brief,' Anne said.

'MacMahon's away so I left the message for the detective-sergeant.'

'Thankfully? . . . Look, my love, stop questioning and criticizing yourself. You've done the right thing, the only thing.'

He wished he could be half as certain as she was.

CHAPTER 19

Ridley read the message and swore. Rickmore was going back on his evidence. And without that, the case was a non-starter. The lever had worked. Elham was proving once again that money and power were what really mattered in life; if you possessed them, you could kick the rest of the world in the goolies; if you possessed them, you could distort and cheat justice . . .

But, he thought, maybe this time it would turn out to be not quite so straightforward as the bastard imagined. He'd gone to considerable trouble to set up that lever to force Rickmore to recant or, if he wouldn't, to destroy his value as a witness. Might he not have gone a little too far? Clever men were sometimes too clever for their own health . . . By God, he'd get Elham yet! Or if he couldn't, he'd make Rickmore curse the day he'd recanted.

It was the first time that Rickmore had entered the divisional HQ, situated at the back of the parish church and in such hideous architectural conflict with it. He was conscious that he was breathing quickly and sweating. Like visiting the dentist, he thought.

There was a counter at one end of the front room and this was manned by a sergeant and a PC. He spoke to the PC.

'Detective-Sergeant Ridley? I'll tell him you're here, Mr Rickmore. If you'll just sit over there until I can find him.'

At the opposite end to the counter were padded wall seats, a few rather spartan chairs, and two tables on which were several magazines, some with direct connection with the police force, and several pamphlets aimed at helping and advising the general public.

He was reading—and hardly taking in—a pamphlet detailing some of the measures a householder could take to protect his home when he heard someone approaching and he looked up to see Ridley.

''Morning, Mr Rickmore. Nice of you to come along.'

He had expected resentment, but Ridley had sounded pleasant.

'I've found an interview room that's free, so let's go along there.'

They left and went down a corridor to the second of three rooms off to the right. It was small, with a single window high up which was barred; the only furniture was a table and six chairs.

'Not the Ritz,' said Ridley, 'but it's quiet . . . Now, about this message—I thought it would be best if you came along and explained things personally.' He produced a pack of cigarettes. 'D'you use these?'

'No, thanks.'

'I wish I could say the same.' He tapped out a cigarette, but before he had time to light it there was a knock on the door and a PC looked in. 'D'you want a cuppa, skipper?'

Ridley turned to Rickmore: 'Which do you drink, tea or coffee?'

'I prefer coffee.'

He said to the PC. 'Two coffees. And get 'em from the canteen, not that flaming machine that can't tell the difference.'

The PC withdrew and shut the door.

Ridley had brought a folder with him and he now opened this and read the top sheet of paper. 'Your message said that you'd made a mistake over your evidence concerning the damage to the Jaguar and the garage. Would you like to be specific?'

Elham had advised him very carefully what to say. He was not to admit to making too direct a mistake; rather, he was to blame the surrounding circumstances. That way, his change of testimony would be very difficult to challenge in court, should he still be called for the prosecution and named a hostile witness. He took a deep breath. 'This last Saturday night my wife and I had dinner at Popham House. We arrived after dark and parked directly in front of the garage because I knew my brother-in-law wouldn't be going out.'

'Just one moment. As I remember it, that's a fairly large garage, so opposite which part of it were you?'

'Well over to the right. We left the car and were moving towards the house when my wife suddenly remembered that we'd forgotten to pick up a magazine we'd brought over for my sister-in-law, so I started back and then happened to glance at the front end of my car and I was convinced there was a dent in the bonnet which hadn't been there before. Yet when I checked, there wasn't anything and I realized it had been a trick of light.'

'When you say light, does that mean that the outside lights of the garage were switched on?'

'Two were, but a third one wasn't working. It was obviously the mixture of shadow and light which had given the impression of a dent.'

'But I seem to remember you saying originally that all three outside lights were working on the night the accident took place?'

'I'm certain I didn't say one way or the other. In fact, one wasn't, just as it wasn't on Saturday. Terence says it's got one of those irritating faults where sometimes it works and sometimes it doesn't. And every time he decides to call in an electrician, it starts behaving itself again.'

The PC returned, carrying a tray on which were two mugs, a teaspoon, and a bowl of sugar. He put the tray in front of Ridley, then left. Ridley pushed the tray to the middle of the table. 'Help yourself.' After Rickmore had taken one mug, Ridley spooned sugar into the second one and then drank. 'Today, it doesn't taste of either tea or coffee.'

Rickmore smiled.

'At least it's hot . . . Getting back to the accident. Originally, you said the offside light was smashed.'

'I said it wasn't working.'

'Both Mr MacMahon and I heard you say that it was smashed.'

'Whatever you heard, that's not what I was trying to say. After all, I didn't go round the bonnet, so there's no way I could have known how it was.'

'Then how did you know the light wasn't working?'

'The headlights were switched on; the offside one wouldn't come on.'

'Why were they switched on if the car was parked?'

'Terence was trying to see if he could get the offside one to work. Personally, I think that that was being rather unrealistically optimistic. He's about as good an electrician as I am mechanic.'

'Do you know if the light failed on the journey back?'

'It went just before they reached our place before dinner.'

'But you told us that when the car left your house, it was unmarked and undamaged.'

'It was. A malfunctioning light isn't damage; that connotes some structural fault.'

'Somewhat pedantic, surely?' said Ridley, not as lightly as he'd intended.

'I'm sorry. Anne says I'm becoming more and more pedantic; one of the penalties of growing older.'

'Or of trying to explain away the difference between what you are saying now and what you said originally?'

'That's nonsense. I haven't changed a thing.'

'Tell me, don't you think it strange how many lights failed that night?'

'Sod's Law. Things never go wrong singly. That's why, if I break something I hurry to break two matches as well.'

Ridley shut the folder. 'Do you realize the full import of what you've just told me?'

'In what way?'

'Your evidence was central to proving your brother-in-law

was driving the car which hit and killed Tamworth. Now, you're denying all you said before.'

'I'm denying nothing that doesn't need to be denied because of the facts.'

'Facts?'

'Yes.'

'Not very pedantic when it comes to the truth?'

Rickmore didn't bother to answer.

'How much did Mr Elham drink at your house that Wednesday night?'

'As far as I can remember, the same as I did. Which was one drink before the meal and a couple of glasses of wine with it.'

'That seems considerably less than your previous estimate.'

'I talked it over with my wife and she has a much better memory than I.'

'So if I asked her, she'd say the same?'

'Yes.'

'As, no doubt, would Mr Elham?'

'I can't answer for him.'

'I expect you can,' said Ridley, no longer bothering to sound pleasant.

Rickmore waited, then said: 'Is there anything more I can tell you?'

'A hell of a lot. But I'm certain you won't.'

'Then I think I ought to get back to work.' Rickmore stood.

'It's a funny thing,' said Ridley, 'how your type always thinks that you've a divine right to escape consequences . . . It must come as a hell of a shock when you discover you haven't.'

As Rickmore went down the passage and into the front room, he wondered uneasily why at the very end there had been an abrupt change of tone in the detective-sergeant's voice—almost as if he'd remembered he'd reason to gloat. He left the building to find that the clouds had lifted and there was some weak sunshine.

Back in the interview room, Ridley used his handkerchief to pick up the mug from which Rickmore had drunk and pack it in a cardboard box, carefully wedging it in place with pieces of foam. He carried the box up to the DI's office. A couple of minutes later, the PC who'd brought the coffee into the interview room, entered. 'Got him as he was leaving, skipper.'

'Let's see it.' The PC handed him a Polaroid snap. Rickmore was three-parts full face on to the camera. It was a good, clear snap.

Unusually, but as previously arranged, Rickmore returned home for lunch. When Anne met him in the hall, she studied his face. 'How did it go?'

'Not nearly as bad as I'd feared.'

'Thank goodness for that . . . Tell me exactly what happened.'

'Over a drink. It may not be the weekend, but I need a strong one.'

'Then have two. The meal's Cumberland hotpot, so it won't spoil.'

He poured out a gin and tonic and a sherry and they settled in the sitting-room. 'Ridley didn't start shouting, or anything like that. In fact, right until the end he seemed to be taking it all in his stride. Then he did show his teeth; said that my sort thought we'd a divine right to escape consequences.'

'If only he'd known a bit more.'

'"Whose conscience with injustice is corrupted."'

She shrugged her shoulders impatiently. 'Did he believe you?'

'Not for one second. Terence said he wouldn't. But apparently they're so used to witnesses going back on their evidence that they learn to treat it as one of the hazards of the profession. My job wasn't to convince him, it was to convince him that I'd be able to convince a jury I was telling the truth.'

'And you think you did that?'

'I'm pretty sure I did.'

'Thank God!'

'I'll drink to that.'

Because Lineport was in a different division, Ridley had first to telephone the local DI and ask permission to carry out the inquiries; on arrival, he had to report to the DI.

'The Guv'nor's been called out,' said the detective-sergeant, 'but he said it's OK to carry on. I've detailed a bloke to go with you.'

'There's no need for anyone.'

He laughed.

The PC who accompanied Ridley was young and quiet and Ridley gained the impression that perhaps he wasn't very smart. That suited him. 'All I'm aiming to do is see whether Chapman can identify from a photo the man who tried to sell him the cup,' he said as they walked briskly up the side road that led into the High Street.

The PC nodded.

'D'you know Chapman?'

'Can't say I do, skipper.'

'So you wouldn't know how quick on the ball he is?'

'No, I wouldn't.'

'Well, we'll sure as hell soon find out, as the young lady said when her boyfriend discovered the rubber was torn.'

The PC hardly smiled.

They entered the antique shop and Ridley introduced himself to Chapman and explained the reason for this visit.

'You want me to recognize him from a photo? I'm afraid

that's going to be difficult. You see, because of that cap he was wearing . . . I believe it has a name, but I don't know what it is.'

'Baseball cap?'

'Perhaps,' he answered doubtfully. 'Certainly, it didn't look very English . . . Anyway, the brim which was very large was pulled right down and the man's moustache was rather large, so much of his face was obscured.'

'But you were able to see his eyes, nose, ears, and chin?'

'I still don't think I'll be able to identify him from a photograph.'

'Have a look at this, will you?' Ridley handed him the Polaroid photograph of Rickmore.

Chapman studied the photograph briefly, then said: 'Just a minute.' He went through to the room behind the counter, returned with a pair of gold-rimmed glasses. He examined the photograph again. 'I can't see any real resemblance.'

'Then I'll just touch things up a bit. Let's have the photo a moment.' Ridley used a pencil to sketch in a baseball cap and a thick moustache. 'Now have another look.'

Chapman studied the photograph a second time. After a while he looked at Ridley over the tops of his spectacles. 'You think this was the man?'

'Let's just say, it's not impossible.'

He held the photograph a little closer. 'It does make quite a difference with the cap and the moustache.'

'Things like that can change a face completely for people who aren't trained observers and who don't know which points to look for. Ears are something which can't be changed. Would you say his ears—' Ridley indicated the photograph—'are similar to those of the man with the cup?'

'They could be.'

'And perhaps the chin's similar?'

'I think it is.'

'And the width of the face at cheekbone level?'

'That's certainly the same.'

'From the sound of things, then he might well . . .' Ridley let his voice die away.

'He might well be the same man. But I still can't be absolutely certain.'

'Never mind. You're saying the next best thing which is that if the man in the photo had a moustache and was wearing a baseball cap, he could very easily have been the man who tried to sell you the cup . . . Thanks very much, Mr Chapman, you've been of great assistance.'

Ridley led the way out of the shop, paused until the traffic eased, then crossed the road and walked briskly along the pavement.

'You were pushing hard, weren't you?' said the PC. 'Out to land Chummy, are you?'

The PC wasn't quite as thick as he'd first judged, thought Ridley. But that didn't really matter. Chapman was the kind of self-opinionated, fussy little man who, now that the seed had been well planted, would swear blind that there was a strong similarity between the two faces.

Because it had been a straight comparison and not a search for which Ridley had called, the fingerprint section were able to report on Tuesday afternoon. Some of the prints on the glass were the same as those on the mug; there were no prints on the bottle.

As Ridley replaced the receiver, he said aloud: 'I've got one of you, you bastards.'

CHAPTER 20

Rickmore was on his feet when he heard the car turn into the drive and he crossed to the window of the sitting-room and parted the curtains. Headlights swept round and then settled on the garage doors, just before being switched off.

'Can you see who it is?' asked Anne. She was knitting a sweater with a complex pattern and the various colours were, temporarily, in something of a cat's-cradle.

'No. Are you expecting someone?'

'Not that I know of.'

He left the sitting-room, switched on the hall and porch lights. He went into the porch and opened the outside door. The light drizzle had stopped, but the wind was damp, suggesting there was more rain to come; not a night for tramps or bald ducks, as his father would have said. He heard the squeal of the garden gate's hinges, then a few seconds later, Ridley came into view.

Ridley came to a stop. ''Evening.' There was no missing his cockiness. 'Got time for a bit of a chat, have you?'

'You'd better come in.' Once Ridley was in the hall, he offered to hang up the sergeant's short overcoat.

'That's very kind of you.' Now there was mockery as well as cockiness.

After hanging up the overcoat, Rickmore said: 'I'll just tell my wife what's happening and then we can go into the dining-room.' He went into the sitting-room and carefully closed the door behind him. 'It's the detective-sergeant. He wants a word. We can go into the dining-room . . .'

'No,' she said. He was trying to shield her from whatever trouble this visit was bringing and she was determined not to be shielded. 'Bring him in here—it's so much warmer.'

He hesitated, then finally nodded. He called Ridley into the room. Ridley said good-evening to Anne with exaggerated politeness. He sat on the settee, faced the fire, and remarked on how much heat it was giving out—he wished the fire in his house was half as good. It became obvious that he was savouring every minute of the run-in to whatever had brought him here.

Rickmore brought an end to the social chit-chat. He said, speaking tightly: 'You wanted a word about something?'

'That's right. About whether you feel like changing the evidence you gave at the station yesterday.'

'No, I don't.'

'You are quite certain?'

'I told you precisely what happened and there's nothing to change. And with regard to thinking I saw a dent in our car, my wife will confirm it all.'

'I'm sure she will. She'll confirm anything to help her brother-in-law escape conviction for running a man down and injuring him so badly that he later died, when he was too tight to know what he was doing.'

'What the devil do you mean?' Rickmore tried to sound indignant, rather than scared.

'I mean that we're not the simple fools you take us for. We know that originally you told us the truth, but now you're lying as hard as you can go.'

'You've no right to come into our house and talk like that,' said Anne fiercely.

'No right? No right when I'm faced by people who are supposed to be law-abiding and an example to the proles like me and I find 'em desperately trying to help one of their own kind escape the consequences of his drunken driving and cowardice?'

Anne spoke to Rickmore. 'You'd better telephone Mr Archer and ask him to drive over here right away.'

'Would that be Mr Archer, the solicitor?' asked Ridley. 'By all means telephone him and tell him to come here. That is, if you don't mind seeing your husband end up in prison.'

'What do you mean by that?'

'Exactly what I said.'

'He's done nothing.'

'Come off it, missus. He's lied his head off.'

'Sergeant,' said Rickmore angrily, 'I don't know what the hell you think you're at, but I do know you're not coming into my house and insulting my wife. Get out. And tomorrow I'll make an official complaint about your behaviour.'

'Sure. Maybe it'll make you feel good. Only perhaps I ought to tell you that complaints from someone about to be indicted for burglary don't cut much ice.'

'Indicted for burglary—are you crazy?'

'D'you know a man called Reginald Gilles? Ever been to his house?'

'And if I have?'

'It was burgled last Wednesday by someone who ought to have been wearing L-plates. Left a footprint in a flowerbed as clear as crystal, broke a pane of glass to force a window, nicked some cups and medals the old boy had won at running, but couldn't open a safe that only called for a bent hatpin. Then on Saturday he tried to sell one of the stolen cups to an antique shop in Lineport. The evidence says it was you who did that job.'

'That's utterly absurd.'

'Is it? Item. What size shoe d'you wear?'

'What's it matter what size?'

'Scared of answering?'

'Ten and a half,' snapped Anne.

Ridley smiled. 'Item. Chummy left a handkerchief with a laundry mark behind. That mark is yours.'

'It can't be . . .' began Rickmore.

'It is. Item. The intruder poured himself a drink to calm his nerves. Your fingerprints are on the glass.'

'They can't possibly have been mine.'

'Then the impossible's happened. Item. When you left the police station, a photograph of you was taken. After a moustache and a baseball cap were shaded in, the owner of the antique shop identified the person in the photo as the man who'd tried to sell him the stolen cup.'

'I haven't been in an antique shop in Lineport in the last couple of years.'

Anne said sharply. 'When was the burglary at Mr Gilles's house?'

'Last Wednesday.'

'I meant, at what time?'

'There's no saying. He went to bed around ten and got up at eight. So it was somewhere between those times.'

'On Wednesday, my husband was here all night.'

'So who's going to alibi him?'

'I am.'

'It's funny, but a wife's alibi never kind of rings very true.'

'He was here all night . . . Damnit, can't you see how ridiculous it is to claim my husband committed a burglary? People like him don't do that sort of thing.'

'If you were to ask me, I'd say that these days there's no knowing who'll do what. After all, there are people like him who drink too much, drive, knock someone over, and haven't the courage to stop and see how badly the victim's injured and if there's anything can be done for him.'

'That . . . that's different.'

'To whom? The victim?'

'You're trying to say Dennis has done something which is totally absurd. How can you begin to believe he'd commit a burglary in the house of someone we know?'

'Meaning he would in the house of someone you didn't know?'

'That's deliberately twisting what I said.' She forced herself to speak more calmly. 'Why would he ever do such a thing?'

'Ask him, not me.'

'You're determined not to understand . . .' She stopped, swung round to face her husband and stared at him for several seconds before she said: 'When was it that I woke up during the night and thought I heard someone downstairs?'

'God knows,' he muttered.

'Wasn't it . . . I know! It was the day I'd been to see Ruth and that was last Wednesday.' Her voice quickened. 'And it was on the Thursday that I couldn't find the handkerchief. You remember, I asked you about it.' She turned back to Ridley. 'What kind of handkerchief was it that was found in the house?'

'It was striped, in three colours; grey, chocolate, and light green.'

'That's the one that went missing! Then I did hear someone that night! And he stole the handkerchief and a glass with Dennis's fingerprints on it and left them at Reggie's house. He was trying deliberately to inculpate Dennis . . . You must see that that's what happened.'

'Must I?'

Rickmore said: 'You're obviously not surprised.'

Ridley did not answer.

'You know very well that I couldn't have carried out that burglary, whatever the evidence suggested. So why try and make out you believe I did?'

Ridley spoke contemptuously. 'You still can't read the score, can you? Not up in the art of self-survival; always had someone ready to come to the rescue . . . Your brother-in-law's a smart lawyer so it didn't take him any time at all to realize that if you persisted in standing by your original evidence, there was sufficient additional circumstantial evidence to nail him; that meant the end of his lifestyle. Equally, he could judge that if you could be persuaded to go back on your evidence, the circumstantial evidence on its own wouldn't be strong enough for him to be charged. So he did everything he could to persuade you to go back on what you'd told us. The trouble was, though, that you were so jealous of him, you wouldn't . . .'

'That's not true,' Anne cried sharply.

Ridley shrugged his shoulders. 'He reckoned your husband was and that's what counted.'

'It was a matter of principle. There are still people who have principles.'

'Sure. Just so long as they don't become inconvenient.'

'You don't know much about people, do you?'

'Mrs Rickmore, after you've been a copper for as long as I have, you know too much about people ever to believe in any of 'em again . . .' He turned to Rickmore. 'Since he wasn't getting anywhere asking, your brother-in-law set about saving himself in the only way left open to him—to destroy your value as a witness. That's why he found someone to set you up for a burglary.'

'He'd never have done such a thing,' said Anne.

'He'd have done anything to anybody to save his own skin.'

'Oh God, you've got a filthy mind!'

'Maybe. But I'll tell you one thing. I respect the law, not treat it with contempt.'

'My husband respects it just as much; maybe more.'

Ridley smiled. 'You could have fooled me, missus . . . Neither of you knew about the burglary before I told you, so Elham hasn't put the screws on you. Why go to all the trouble of fixing the burglary if not to use it? Obviously, because in the event he didn't need to. Why? Because after he'd set things rolling, the dead man was identified as a rapist and suddenly your principles weren't important enough. Like I said, people only hold principles until they become inconvenient.'

Rickmore bitterly acknowledged that in the present context, this was true.

'You decided to agree to go back on your evidence. So now there's no firm case against your brother-in-law, unless . . .'

'Unless what?'

'You decide to tell the truth after all.'

'I've told you the truth.'

'You told me a pack of bloody lies.'

'I swear it was the truth.'

Ridley said with pleasure: 'Still not understood? Not realized that when he set out to fix you for burglary, your brother-in-law did a good job; too good a job. If all the evidence is presented, you're going to go on trial and you're going to be found guilty.'

'That can't happen now,' said Anne.

'Why not?'

'You've admitted you don't believe Dennis had anything to do with it.'

'What I believe is immaterial; it's the evidence that counts. It always is.'

'But you know that he's innocent.'

'Strange how things work out, isn't it? You were ready to see someone guilty be found innocent, but now you're screaming because someone innocent may be found guilty.' He paused, then added: 'I hope you noticed I said "may be", not "is going to be".'

'What are you getting at now?' demanded Rickmore.

'Tell the truth about your brother-in-law and you won't be put on trial for burglary.'

'You're trying to blackmail me.'

'Blackmail, hell. I'm offering you a choice.'

'You're no better than the crooks you're meant to catch,' said Anne.

Ridley's anger finally overflowed. 'Me? All I want is to see justice done. But you lot—you want to bury justice. So who is it who's no bloody better than the villains?'

CHAPTER 21

Rickmore braked the Escort to a halt outside the garage of Popham House. Anne put her hand on his left arm. 'Don't lose your temper.'

'Do you know what I'd like to do . . .'

'Yes. But don't.'

'He doesn't give one solitary damn for anyone but himself. He'd see me jailed and our lives ruined, if that meant he could escape the consequences of his own drunkenness. He hasn't the guts to face . . .'

'I know all that, but I also know that if you lose your temper, as you can do when you're really worked up, you won't accomplish anything.'

A man who abhorred violence, no matter what the cause, he would have inflicted violence on Elham without a second's thought because, by his actions, Elham was threatening Anne.

She said quietly: 'If Terence knows the police have told us the facts, I'm sure he'll admit the truth. He can't have thought it would get to the point where you might actually be charged with burglary; all he was trying to do was destroy your potential value as a prosecution witness in the eyes of the police.'

'You'd have found an excuse for Judas Iscariot.' He climbed out of the car.

She joined him and linked her arm with his. 'Remember, count ten before you say anything.'

'I'll need a goddamn calculator.'

Penelope was in the kitchen and she greeted them with warmth, twice saying how nice it was to see them again so soon; but she could not hide her apprehension in the face of Rickmore's grimness.

'Is Terence back?' he asked.

'Not yet; he phoned to say he'd be catching the later train.' She looked up at the wall clock. 'But he shouldn't be long now. Let's go through and have a drink. And you will stay to supper, won't you?'

'No.'

'But you must; honestly, there's masses of food because I ordered a sirloin and the butcher must have thought we were entertaining an army. Terence so dislikes cold meat and if you don't eat with us, I don't know what I'll do with it all.'

'We can't stay.'

She nibbled her lower lip and looked at her sister, but merely gained confirmation that something was very, very wrong. 'I . . . Let's go through.'

They had been in the blue sitting-room less than ten minutes when they heard a car door slam. 'I'll go and tell him you're here.' Penelope hurried out.

A couple of minutes later, Elham, in black coat and striped trousers, entered the sitting-room, closely followed by Penelope. ''Evening, Anne; 'Evening, Dennis.' His manner was watchful, but not fearful, as was his wife's. 'Either of you ready for a refill while I get a drink for myself.'

'No, thanks,' answered Rickmore curtly.

'I'd like another vodka and tonic,' said Penelope hurriedly.

He took her glass and left. When he returned, and after handing her one glass, he moved to his favoured position in front of the fire.

'We had the detective-sergeant round at our place again,' said Rickmore.

'What did he want?'

'To tell me that you had done your damnedest to destroy

my value as a witness if I refused to change my original evidence; to tell me that you'd been a bit too clever before we learned the dead man was a rapist, and now the evidence against me is so strong that if I don't change my story back to what it was, I'll be on a charge of burglary and he'll personally guarantee that I'm found guilty.'

'God Almighty!'

'Don't bother to try to sound surprised and outraged . . .'

'You surely don't think that there's any truth in all that?'

'I'd say there's quite a bit.'

'You really believe I'd deliberately let you be falsely accused of a crime?'

'If it got you off a charge.'

'I promise you I had nothing to do with this. I know absolutely nothing about it . . . Did the detective-sergeant detail the evidence?'

'You don't remember what it was? The handkerchief, the glass with my prints on it, the attempt to sell the cup stolen from Reggie Gilles.'

'What cup was stolen from Reggie? What d'you mean by the handkerchief and the glass?'

'Forget the innocent act. Who else is going to bother to try to destroy my character? Who else stands to gain if it is destroyed? No one.'

'Tell me all the facts.'

'You bloody well know them better than I do.'

'I know nothing.'

He didn't want to believe Elham, yet the other's quiet sincerity, following a bewildered amazement that surely would have been difficult to simulate, began to undermine his certainty.

'What exactly did the detective say?'

Rickmore stared at him, still unwilling to admit his accusations might be unfounded, and it was Anne who answered.

Elham listened, saying nothing until she'd finished. 'You

definitely heard someone in the house that night?'

'No. If I'd been certain, I'd have woken Dennis. There was just this noise which wasn't repeated.'

'Did you miss a glass as well as a handkerchief?'

She shrugged her shoulders. 'I can't say how many glasses of each kind we should have; not to the nearest one. You know how it goes—some are smashed and get replaced, some don't—one just doesn't keep count of everyday drinking glasses.'

'Did the detective-sergeant indicate how strong an identification the owner of the antique shop made and how he made it?'

'As far as I can remember, he told us he'd got a photo of Dennis and when a cap and a moustache were shaded in, the owner identified the photo as being of the man who'd tried to sell him the cup.'

'Did he say anything to suggest that the owner was offered several photos of different people to choose from and he picked out this one?'

'I don't think so.' She looked at Rickmore and he shook his head.

Elham drained his glass, put it down on the table, began to pace the floor, passing between his wife and Anne. After a while, he came to a stop and faced Rickmore. 'I swear I did not have anything at all to do with this burglary—that was clearly designed to destroy your credibility as a witness.'

'Who else would have fixed it?'

'Precisely. When the only possible motive uniquely concerns myself . . . It could only have been one person.'

Elham entered chambers and stood in the doorway of the clerks' room. Arnold was on the phone, Betty was typing. ''Morning, Mr Elham,' she said.

''Morning. Tell Tom I want a word with him as soon as he's finished.'

She showed her surprise at so unnecessary an instruction —Arnold always reported in the morning.

In his room, Elham crossed to the window and looked down at the small square. He had no doubts, but until the facts had been confirmed he could not begin to try to find a way out of the seemingly hopeless position in which he and Rickmore now found themselves. If things remained as they were, he would go free, but Rickmore would be charged with burglary and probably be found guilty. He could not and would not let that happen. But the alternative was for him to tell the truth about the accident and then he himself would be on a criminal charge. He dare not let that happen . . .

Arnold entered the room. 'Good morning, sir.'

Arnold was looking old, Elham thought, yet he was not quite sixty. But then he'd probably never looked young. 'Sit down.' He walked over to his desk.

Arnold moved one of the chairs and set it in front of the desk.

Elham said: 'You fixed for someone to fake evidence which would inculpate my brother-in-law on a charge of burglary.'

There was a long silence.

'Didn't you?'

'I had to,' Arnold replied, pleading for understanding. 'I had to try to make certain that if he went into court, the jury wouldn't believe him.'

'Who planted the evidence?'

'A man called Dean. Two years ago, Mr Vernay defended him and got him off, against the evidence. He was so pleased that he said if either of us ever needed help, we had only to ask.'

'You told him what to do?'

'Yes. I tried very hard to work out how best to arrange things.'

'And succeeded a damned sight too well.'

'How d'you mean?'

'Mr Rickmore, when he learned the dead man was a rapist, decided to change his evidence . . .'

'To . . . to change it?'

'In my favour. But now the evidence you had planted is strong enough to have Mr Rickmore found guilty, despite the inherent unlikelihood of someone in his position turning to burglary.'

Arnold was uninterested in Rickmore's problems.

'So now either he tells the truth and I end up in court, or he doesn't and he ends up in court.'

'You?'

'Yes.'

'You can't . . .'

'I can't keep quiet and see him jailed.'

Arnold struggled to understand this sudden development, one he had entirely failed to foresee. He stared with anguish at Elham. 'I didn't . . . I didn't realize . . . I'll go to the police and tell them what I've done.'

'Then you'll have to explain about the car accident as well as the burglary, since your confession can only carry validity if your motive's fully explained.'

'But . . . but . . .'

'And do you think that anyone, in the light of all the facts as others will see them, will ever believe you acted entirely on your own initiative? The net result of your going to the police would just be a further charge of attempting to pervert the course of justice.'

'Then what am I to do?'

'God knows! But if you get any bright ideas, tell me what they are before you do anything . . . That's all.'

Arnold stared beseechingly at Elham, then stood and shuffled out of the room.

Elham returned to the window and once more stared

down at the square. A man, red bag in his hand, was just passing out of sight through the archway at the far end. Tewksbury-Smith, thought Elham, identifying him by the very characteristic way in which he walked with his head thrown back. A contemporary, whose career his own had closely parallelled, even to the fact that he was taking Silk at the same time . . . Or would have been, had the rapist not suddenly run out on to the road in a scene that was replayed again and again in his tortured mind . . . Again and again. Again and again. Had he discovered a way of escape?

CHAPTER 22

The rain, driven by a north-east wind, beat against the window of the sitting-room of Oak Tree Cottage. Intermittently, there was the teeth-twitching sound of an unpruned rose trail scratching at the glass.

They heard neither the rain nor the rose trail; only Elham as he explained the situation.

'That's how things stand,' he said finally. He took a handkerchief from his pocket and lightly wiped his mouth.

Rickmore was silent for a while, then he said: 'If your chief clerk confesses to the police what really happened, I'll be in the clear?'

'You would be, if he were believed.'

'Why shouldn't he be?'

'Because Dean, the man who carried out the burglary, will naturally deny everything and then Arnold's evidence will be uncorroborated. In those circumstances, he'll only be believed if his motive is obviously strong enough to make it likely he's telling the truth.'

'In other words, if he says he did it in order to incriminate me so that my evidence against you wouldn't be believed?'

'Yes.'

'Which makes it obvious that it was your car which ran down the rapist?'

'Yes.'

'Then what you're really saying is that one of us will be prosecuted?'

'On the face of things.' He paused, then said, very hurriedly: 'But so that there's no room for doubt, if one of us is to be prosecuted, I will make quite certain that it is not you.'

'I don't understand,' said Anne. 'One moment you say it has to be one or other of you, the next you say "if" it is.'

'A criminal case is usually concerned very much more with the evidence than the law, as opposed, for instance, to a complicated company case. The laws of evidence—which among other things lay down what is and what is not admissible—are very arcane and even to us lawyers not always certain. Added to this is the fact that the evidence often does not carry in the minds of the jurors the weight it should and would in an ordered and trained mind. That's why there'll often be a situation where the police are properly satisfied a man committed a crime, but the case never appears in court. Bitter experience has shown them that it's certain either some vital piece of evidence will be held to be inadmissible, or the jury, with their untrained, emotional, and frequently illogical minds, will incorrectly interpret the evidence in the accused's favour. Because of this, I think . . .' He stopped.

'You think what?'

'I think the value of the evidence against you can be undermined.'

'How?'

'By making certain it would be incorrectly interpreted in your favour.'

'That's impossible. When the detective listed it all, he almost had me believing I must have done it.'

'Difficult, not impossible.' He was plainly nervous and uncertain and there was a suggestion of humility in his manner. 'There is one way in which both of us can escape prosecution. But it would mean your taking a risk.'

'Both of us escape?'

'If it's certain the DPP would decide it would be stupid to bring a charge of burglary against you because no jury would ever find you guilty, the police won't be able to blackmail you into telling the truth about the night of the accident.'

'How much of a risk?' demanded Anne.

'Probably very little. Obviously, though, something can always go wrong.'

'What are you asking Dennis to do?'

Elham did not immediately answer her. He faced Rickmore and spoke quickly. 'I know we've never got on too well together. And so maybe you'd rather not risk anything. If so, I've told you, I'll tell the police the truth about the accident. But if you could do this . . .' He came to a stop. He was unwilling to plead any further, not because of pride, but because he did not want to seem to be using emotional pressure to persuade.

Anne looked at Rickmore and it was that look, more than anything Elham had said, which decided him. 'I'll give it a go.'

Rickmore had read many personal accounts of going into battle and he had often wondered how he would feel in the moments immediately before an action began. Now he thought he knew. Sick with fear.

He hid the bicycle in a clump of brambles and then listened for any sounds which might suggest that he had been spotted. He discovered that the night had a thousand tongues. A sound to the right convinced him all was over before it had begun; but the sound was repeated and he now identified it as some small animal, frantically scuttling away. Seconds later, a more distant sound made him freeze, but that turned out to be a bulling cow, declaring her passion. He shifted his weight and a twig snapped, sounding to his straining ears like a rifle shot . . .

He moved forward and almost tripped as a bramble trail caught his right foot. When he regained his balance, he could feel the sweat under his armpits. He'd been crazy to agree to this nightmare. He hadn't been under any obligation. Dammit, he didn't even like Elham. Elham had shown himself to be a coward and a traitor, ready to betray the law he served . . . Rickmore's right hand, which he'd been holding out in front of him, banged into the bole of a tree and he exclaimed aloud from the shock, not the very brief pain. Christ! he thought, a fool hits not the same tree that a wise man sees.

He briefly shone the torch ahead of him, the bowl carefully masked with tape to narrow the beam. Immediately to his right was the tree he'd just encountered, five feet further on was a hedge, beautifully cut and laid. So he'd reached the edge of the rough land and ahead was the field which led up to the garden of Heskthorne House.

Elham had said that the Moffats were on holiday in France. He hoped to God that was right. He'd only met Moffat once, but that had been sufficient to convince him that he was a man who'd pull both triggers of a twelve-bore before he asked what the intruder wanted.

He clambered over the hedge, snagging his trousers on one of the uprights around which the laid branches were woven. He moved forward into the field and there was a snort from his right and the sounds of several animals moving. Cows. He remembered the friend of Anne's whose herd of Ayrshires had suddenly and for no discernible reason attacked her, inflicting serious injuries. His mind had become a forcing ground for catastrophes.

The field was not large and he soon reached the tall yew hedge which surrounded the garden. A hundred yards to the right was a wooden gate, and looking over this he could see the black bulk of the house, just discernible against the clear, star-studded sky. There was a light on upstairs. Elham had said that there would be. The Moffats used time-switches in different parts of the house to give the impression of active habitation. But what if this light had not been activated by a time-switch, but by someone brought in to house-sit . . . ?

He pulled on a pair of gloves, opened the gate, and passed through. A grass verge ran the length of the kitchen garden and ended at a gravel path; just before the path, he carefully left a firm footprint in the rich loam. Then he crossed the path as carefully as he could, yet still making so much noise that he doubted whether an elephant could have made more.

To the right of the kitchen door was a window, some four feet above the ground. He picked up a stone and, praying that it was true that the kitchen lay outside the alarm system, threw it through the glass. The explosion of noise terrified him, but after it was over there was nothing to suggest it had alarmed anyone. He knocked away a couple of dangerous slivers of glass, then reached in and pushed the catch up so that the window could be opened inwards. He climbed over the sill. And as he stood in the kitchen, the unwelcome thought came to him of how ironic it was that he, a man who had always believed in the law, should now be committing burglary . . .

Elham had described the alarm system, explaining that Moffat had asked him what kind to install and he had suggested the same make and type as was in Popham House.

The kitchen was large and equipped with every conceivable piece of electrical equipment, including an extremely large refrigerator of American make. Immediately to the left of this was a built-in cupboard and in the cupboard was a wooden box which contained two switches, two pilot lights, one red, one green, and ten numbered buttons like those found on a simple pocket calculator. To de-activate the alarm system, which sounded not only in the house but also in the nearest police station, it was necessary to punch in a six-figure code before pushing one switch up and the other down. Get the code wrong and within minutes a police car would arrive . . . Moffat, a man with a very poor memory, had—so Elham swore—chosen the numbers of his birthday. Rickmore punched out one four one ten one seven. The green light went out, the red one came on. He pressed one switch up, the other down, reversing the positions in which they had been.

Mouth dry, heart thumping, he crossed to the far door and opened this. The alarm stayed silent. He stepped into the passage.

Moffat had been an administrator in the Colonial Service —which explained his aggressive manner—and when in West Africa he'd made a small but good collection of carved wooden masks which now hung on the walls of the sitting-room; Rickmore picked off the two smallest ones and put them on a chair. At the far end of the room, to the left of the fireplace, was a cupboard and on the shelves of this was a wide selection of bottles and glasses. He chose a bottle of Glenfiddich and put it on an unusually shaped table, carved out of a single piece of heavily grained wood. He brought from his coat pocket a glass which had been protected with bubbled plastic wrapping. He unwrapped the glass and placed it by the bottle, returned the wrapping to his pocket, poured just enough whisky into the glass to make it appear it had been used.

The library was traditional in style, with two alcoves. The safe was in one of the alcoves, concealed by panelling which matched that around the rest of the room. He left the concealing wooden door open. Finally, he dropped a handkerchief near the beautifully inlaid partner's desk.

After collecting up the two wooden masks, he returned to the kitchen. He crossed to the alarm control box and reversed the positions of the switches; the red light went out and the green one came on.

He went over to the door leading into the passageway he'd just come down, took a very deep breath, and opened the door. Immediately, the alarm sounded.

He left the house, assuring himself that more haste meant less speed, but nevertheless moving far more quickly than conditions—but not the thought of the approaching police car—warranted.

The gates of Popham House were shut, but not locked, and he opened the right-hand one and wheeled the bike through. Keeping within the cover of the garage—to obviate the very slight risk that one of the Cavajals was awake and looking out of a window—he returned the bike to the small lumber room at the back of the garage.

Elham, his face puffy from tension, met him in the kitchen. 'Well?' he demanded hoarsely.

'I've grown a wonderful crop of ulcers, but there was no alarm until the end.'

'Thank God!'

'Where's Anne?'

'I tried to persuade her to go to bed, but she wouldn't. She's fallen asleep on the settee.'

'Then I'll wake her up and inform her that she won't have to visit me in jail in the morning . . . But first, I could use a whisky in the biggest glass you've got.'

Elham's need was no less.

CHAPTER 23

DC Wrybot—his surname was a constant source of childish ribaldy in the CID general room—entered the DI's room. ''Morning, skipper.'

'If you insist,' muttered Ridley, who had had a heavy night with his wife and two other married couples.

'I thought you'd want to know that there was a break-in at Polhurst last night.'

'So why get excited?'

'The property belongs to Moffat, who they say is some sort of bigwig on the county council.'

Ridley swore. 'And I suppose now he's yelling blue murder and wants the whole bloody Force switched to his case?'

'Probably would if he knew about it, but he's on holiday in France somewhere. The lucky sod.'

'Was much nicked?'

'There's been no word through on that yet.'

'Find out.'

'But I am busy . . .'

'Do as you're told without bloody arguing.'

Pardon me for living, thought Wrybot, as he left.

County HQ rang to ask why hadn't they received the weekly T254 forms? Ridley replied that he'd posted them the previous evening, as he stared at them by the side of the blotter. After the call was over, he began to fill them in. He no longer wondered why MacMahon had always looked harassed. He'd been working for less than five minutes when the telephone rang again. He swore, but it kept on ringing.

'Midge here, skipper,' said Wrybot. 'I'm phoning from Heskthorne House. According to the daily, all that was nicked was two wooden masks that were hanging on the wall. Bloody ugly things if they were anything like the ones that are left. Anyway, that's all she can tell us about and it doesn't look as if we'll know any more until the owners get back. Chummy found the safe, with the family jewels inside —so the daily says—but he didn't do anything about it. And that's odd, really, since a sectional jemmy would have opened it up as easy as you like.'

A thought began to form in Ridley's mind, but then Wrybot spoke again and the thought failed to coalesce.

'He was either cool or bloody nervous. Helped himself to a whisky; Glenfiddich, no less!' Wrybot chuckled. 'Cool or nervous, he was careless. They found a hankie near the desk in the library and the daily swears it's nothing to do with her and wasn't there the last time she did that room.'

Ridley suddenly realized what that half-formed thought a moment ago had been signposting. 'Is there a laundry mark?'

'As a matter of fact, yeah, there is. I was just about to say . . .'

'Is it R one four four?'

'Jeez . . . How the hell d'you know that?'

'Because I'm bloody psychic, that's how. And I'll tell you something else. Somewhere outside, there's a nice clear footprint of Chummy.'

'If you know it all, skipper, why bother to send me out?'

'Because now you're going to search the place so hard that if a single grain of dust fell off Chummy, you'll find it. I'll send a couple of lads along to help.'

'All this for a job where only a couple of wooden masks have been nicked . . . Skipper, you wouldn't be thinking of standing for the council, would you?'

'Stop trying to be bloody smart . . . And get the bottle of whisky and the glass off to Dabs.'

'Will do . . . By the way, I was due to collect a couple of

witnesses' statements this morning from over Delsham way. What shall I do about them?'

'Forget 'em.'

'The pleasure's all mine.'

After he'd replaced the receiver, Ridley balled his fist and slammed it down on the desk in a display of impotent anger. This was one move he had not foreseen.

The fingerprint laboratory rang on Wednesday morning. The whisky bottle and glass had been checked for prints and comparison tests had been made. Several prints, from two different persons, were on the bottle; none of them had been made by the named person. The glass had been wiped clean at some recent time and there had been only one set of prints on it; these had been made by the named person.

Ridley turned off the road and into the yard of Oak Tree Cottage, where he parked. He and Wrybot climbed out.

'Neat little place,' said Wrybot, as they began walking. 'Give me half a chance and I'll be living in somewhere like this.' When there was no comment, he looked sideways at the detective-sergeant. Sour, he thought; like the girlfriend's quince jelly.

Ridley opened the gate and led the way round the brick path to the porch. He was about to ring the bell when Anne stepped into the porch and opened the outside door. 'I'd like a word with your husband,' he said curtly. 'I tried to ring him at the office, but they said he was ill.'

'That's right.'

'Not too ill, I imagine, to answer a few questions?'

'I can find out.' She showed them into the sitting-room, carefully reminding them both to duck their heads as they went in and to beware of the central beam once inside. She then offered them coffee, but Rickmore bad-temperedly refused.

'Then do sit down while I go and see how my husband's feeling now.' She left, closing the door behind herself.

Wrybot looked up at the beams. 'I really go for these, skipper.'

'Yeah?'

'It's a bit of history, like.'

'Never could stand the subject.'

Wrybot briefly wondered what was bugging the DS so hard, then let his mind wander. He was on holiday with his girlfriend, enjoying most of the pleasures that life had to offer, when footsteps overhead jerked his mind back to reality. Very soon afterwards, Anne returned with Rickmore who, Wrybot decided, did not look particularly ill.

'Sorry to be a bit of time,' said Rickmore, 'but I was lying down . . . My wife says you've refused coffee. Would you prefer a drink?'

'No, thanks,' replied Ridley, angered by their courtesy. 'We're investigating a burglary which took place on Monday. A house at Polhurst belonging to Sir Rupert Moffat was broken into. Do you know him?'

'We've met him and his wife once, but I think that's all.'

'Did you meet them at their house?'

'No, we've never been there. It was at a home belonging to mutual friends.'

'The intruder smashed a window to get in and then neutralized the alarm system. The method of entry was crude, but the alarm system is sophisticated and to de-activate it one has to punch in six figures on a control board. Obviously, the possible combinations are far too many for anyone to punch in the right one by chance. So the intruder had to know the correct code. This all says something, doesn't it?'

'I'm afraid I don't follow.'

'It says that the intruder didn't know much about house-breaking, but he did know a lot about the Moffats.'

'That sounds logical.'

'He found the safe, but didn't do anything about it. Yet any half-competent peterman with a sectional jemmy would have ripped it open inside five minutes. So he doesn't know much about safe-cracking either. Is this all beginning to sound rather familiar?'

'Should it?'

'He helped himself to a whisky and left the bottle and glass out, making it obvious. He dropped a handkerchief, which happened to have a laundry mark. He planted a footprint in the kitchen garden . . . Now has the penny dropped?'

'It sounds a bit like that other burglary.'

'Exactly similar. And just to make certain we weren't so dumb we didn't get the message, there were fingerprints on the glass.'

'Presumably that makes things easier for you?'

'The laundry mark was yours and the prints were yours.'

'Impossible.'

'Why won't you understand something? I'm not as thick as you'd bloody like me to be. I know that you broke into Heskthorne House, not to nick whatever was going, but to leave those clues.'

'When they appear to inculpate me? I'd have to be mad to do that.'

'Or trying to save both your brother-in-law's and your own skins.'

'How in the wide world do you bring him into it?'

'How d'you bloody think? . . . Understand something. I'm going to prove it was you. Not with the clues you wanted us to find, but with the ones you don't even know about. No one ever goes anywhere, or does anything, without leaving traces; I'll find 'em, if it takes me a bloody month of Sundays.'

'You hate my husband,' said Anne.

About to reply that he'd cause to, Ridley realized just in time that to do so would be both stupid and dangerous.

'You're twisting everything he says.'

'I've stated facts, nothing more.'

'The fact is,' said Rickmore, 'if a glass with my prints on it and a handkerchief with our laundry mark appeared in a house that's been burgled, someone is obviously trying to inculpate me.'

'That was true the first time, but not now. You've deliberately pointed the finger at yourself in the belief that it will never be accepted that anyone in his right senses would deliberately incriminate himself twice.'

'When was this burglary?'

'You know that just as well as me. You re-activated the alarm when you'd finished, to make certain that the police had a time. No doubt you're now going to offer an alibi?'

'I can't answer that until I know the time.'

'A quarter to one on Tuesday morning.' Ridley's voice became thick with sarcasm. 'Presumably you're now going to tell me that your wife will vouch for the fact that you were in this house at that time?'

'No, she won't do that.'

The answer completely surprised him. It was several seconds before he said: 'You don't have an alibi?'

'I do. But not one based on this house. That night, we had dinner at my brother-in-law's and stayed on very late.'

Ridley's confidence returned. 'You're hoping his evidence will carry a bit more weight than your wife's?'

'I imagine so, since his wife was there as well. That makes three people who can vouch that I'm telling the truth.'

'You're so goddamn naïve . . . They've all as much motive to lie as you have. They couldn't alibi Father Christmas.'

'Are you suggesting that not even the evidence of all three of them is sufficient?'

'I'm suggesting exactly that.'

'Then who would satisfy you? St Peter?'

'No need to bother him. Just give me someone who's even half-way independent.'

'How about Arnold?'

'Who?'

'Mr Elham's chief clerk. There was some problem that needed thrashing out, so Arnold came down and stayed at Popham House on Monday night. He and Mr Elham left us after dinner and went up to the study; they didn't come down until considerably later. Then, when we said we ought to go, my brother-in-law said he'd hardly had a chance to have a word with us and he persuaded us to stay on. I don't know what the time was when we left, except it was after one.'

Ridley knew a growing bitter frustration.

CHAPTER 24

A DC from the Metropolitan police telephoned Ridley on Friday. 'Reference your request to question Thomas Arnold. I'm just back from having a word with him. He states categorically that Rickmore and his wife were at Popham House all evening and didn't leave there until sometime after one on Tuesday morning.'

'The bastard's got to be lying.'

There was a short pause, then the DC said: 'He was pretty confident.'

'I don't care how confident, he was bloody lying.' Ridley forced himself to calm down. 'What's he like; how would he make out in a witness-box?'

'He's a funny old boy—all dust and antique. But I reckon if you matched him against a mule, you'd soon hear the mule shout uncle.'

Ridley swore.

*

Mrs MacMahon opened the front door of her house. She smiled. 'Hullo, Steve, nice to see you again. Come to have a word with Jim?'

'If he's up to it?'

'He's much better, especially since they say now that he did have a heart attack, but it was so minor that if he leads a sensible life he won't know any more about it. Of course, being him, he started talking about returning to work immediately, but I soon put a stop to that . . . But come on in instead of standing there and listening to me going on and on. The thing is, it's such a weight off my mind that half the time I feel as if I'd had a fix.' She laughed. 'Jim says I'm acting as giddy as when he first met me. Too much extra weight for anything like that, I told him.'

MacMahon was in the greenhouse in the back garden. 'I'm getting ready for Spring,' he said, pointing to a propagator. He studied Ridley. 'You're beginning to look like a man with responsibilities.'

'Frustrations.'

'The two go together, like corruption and politicians. And the best way of coping with 'em is to have a beer—and a fag, if the wife's not around to see me.'

They went into the kitchen, where MacMahon picked up two cans of beer, and then on through to the sitting-room. He handed Ridley a can. 'You don't mind managing without a glass, I hope? I'm doing the washing-up these days, so I keep it down as far as possible.' He sat, pulled the tab off the can, and drank. 'OK, so what's got you more frustrated than a eunuch in a harem?'

Ridley told him.

'You know something?' said MacMahon. 'You've largely got yourself to blame.'

'What the hell for?'

'For things being as they are now. Remember me saying softlee, softlee?'

'Not that again?'

'You pushed 'em too hard, too quickly. You squeezed 'em into a corner so that they had to do something dramatic if they were to do anything. If you'd moved slowly, maybe appearing a little soft as if you'd not understood what had been going on, they'd have assumed they were safe and their guards would have been down and then, like as not, you'd have been able to dig up something really incriminating that would have nailed Elham.'

Ridley said heatedly: 'You say I've made a balls-up. But it doesn't matter how smart they've been, I'll show 'em I'm smarter. I'll get 'em.'

MacMahon looked quizzically at him, then stood and went over to the low bookshelf which was filled with book-club volumes. He brought out the first three volumes to reveal a pack of cigarettes. He offered this, then helped himself to one, replaced the pack and the books, and returned to his chair after accepting a light from Ridley. 'How?'

'How what?'

'How are you going to get them? How are you going to persuade a jury that any man in his right mind is going to lay a trail that points directly at himself?'

'By setting out the facts.'

MacMahon shook his head.

'Why not?'

'Can you prove Elham was driving the car which ran down Tamworth so long as Rickmore sticks to his present evidence?'

'No.'

'Then you're left with charging Rickmore. At his trial, evidence concerning Elham's hit-and-run is inadmissible. And if you can't show that that's the thread which binds together the hit-and-run case, the burglary at Gilles's place which appeared to have been committed by Rickmore but wasn't, and the burglary at Heskthorne House that was committed by him, you can't begin to offer a logical explanation of why Rickmore should deliberately incriminate himself.'

'It's bloody obvious.'

'To you and me, but not to any jury. And something else. You're faced with an alibi—four people prepared to swear that at the time of the burglary, Rickmore was in Popham House.'

'Four people all with a motive for seeing Rickmore gets off.'

'What are their motives?'

'Rickmore's wife is trying to protect him, Elham wants to save him in case he decides to tell the truth about the hit-and-run case, and Elham's wife is naturally backing up her husband.'

'And Arnold?' MacMahon tapped ash from the cigarette into the palm of his other hand. 'Who's not a relative by blood or marriage so that there's no obvious link to make him lie.'

'He works for Elham.'

'Not strong enough.'

'Well, it's obvious, isn't it? He helped rig the first burglary.'

'How do you go about proving that, which you must do to break the image of him as an independent witness?'

'By showing what . . .' He stopped.

'By showing what was his motive for helping Elham? But such evidence would be inadmissible in a trial of Rickmore for burglary.'

'All right, then,' said Ridley violently, 'add in the first burglary. Between them . . .'

'Put the two together and the proposition that Rickmore's twice left behind the same incriminating evidence becomes patently absurd . . . And, as a matter of interest, would you like to have it brought out in court that you've held back evidence?'

'I've done what?'

'Is it in the official records that the prints on the mug were Rickmore's and they matched the prints on the glasses found at the two burglaries?'

'I . . . Maybe I . . .'

'Maybe you've held that information back, hoping to use it to pressure Rickmore into telling the truth?'

There was a long silence. MacMahon drank some beer. As he put the can down, there was a sound from outside the room and he quickly held the cigarette ready to throw into the fireplace in an attempt to hide from his wife the fact that he had been smoking. But a moment later they heard her go up the stairs and he relaxed. 'There's something else you need to consider. How'd you feel in the witness-box, faced by a counsel determined and delighted to prove how inefficiently you've handled the case?'

'Come off it,' said Ridley angrily.

'Handled inefficiently because you've allowed yourself to be blinded by your dislike of the people involved.'

'What are you getting at?'

'Rickmore's wife spoke of hearing someone in their house on the Wednesday night, the suggestion being that an intruder stole the handkerchief and a glass bearing Rickmore's prints, to plant in Gilles's house. Did you have the other prints on the glass checked to see if they were Mrs Rickmore's?'

'No.'

'Did you check whether the glass matched others in the burgled house, or, alternatively, those in Oak Tree Cottage?'

'No.'

'Remember the bottle? There weren't any prints of Rickmore's on it. Why not? He wasn't wearing gloves when he handled the glass. Presumably, you wouldn't try to suggest that he wore gloves to pick up the bottle, but took them off to pick up the glass?'

'For Christ's sake, which side are you batting for?'

'Although you sound as if you'd have trouble understanding right now, yours. I don't want to see you ruin your career.'

'But you don't mind seeing them get off scot free?'

'They won't.'

'If they never appear in court, they goddamn will.'

MacMahon shook his head. He drank and emptied the can, drew on the cigarette and then leaned over to stub it out in the ashtray that Ridley was using. 'They're not villains, they're just ordinary people who got caught up in a situation where cowardice, stupidity, fear and a mistaken sense of loyalty, drove them to breaking the law. They're people whose entire lives would be shattered by being found guilty of a crime. So from now on they'll be living in fear that one day some extra piece of evidence will come to light that will be enough to shoot one or both of them into court. And on top of that, it's an odd thing, but in my experience people who commit crimes almost always suffer some kind of a loss, never mind what the state does to them. I sometimes think it must be an outside force which makes certain all of us pay a penalty for our misdeeds.'

To Ridley's bitter anger, there was now added contempt for such Holy-Joe philosophy.

It was February 18th. In the main bedroom of Popham House, Penelope drew her dress up over her shoulders, hung it on a hanger, put it in one of the built-in cupboards. Elham, already in bed, watched her and experienced a growing desire. She took off her lace-edged petticoat and dropped this into the Ali-Baba basket by the side of her dressing-table; she never wore underwear more than once. She reached up behind her back and unclipped her brassière, removed it, put it in the hamper. She had pert breasts, with prominent nipples and generous areolæ. He imagined his fingers caressing her nipples and his mouth dried. She slid off her pants and put those in the basket, bent down to pick up the lid which she put in place. Obviously aware of the intensity with which he was regarding her, she walked over to her bed, unzipped the bag in the shape of an elephant, and brought out her frothy and very expensive nightdress.

'Leave that and come over here,' he said thickly.

'No. It's been a heavy day and I'm tired.' She slipped on the nightdress and climbed into bed.

By her actions and the way in which she had spoken, he understood something which should have been clear to him before. Until the accident, he had always been proud of her, not least because she aroused envy in other men, but he had condescendingly assumed his superiority; this superiority had made him the dominant partner. She had accepted her subservience. But after the accident, he had shown himself to be weak and she had proved herself to be strong. His dominion had been destroyed, just as she had ceased to be subservient. And because she had grown strong at his expense, she was now going to deny him her body as well as her passion in revenge for the past.

He stared up at the ceiling and in his mind saw Lucy, naked, passionate, and he knew an impotent desire so strong that it was pain.

Anne said: 'Do I dare risk offering you a penny for them?'

Rickmore jerked his mind back to the present and looked across the sitting-room at her.

'Or are your thoughts too interesting to be traded for sordid money?'

He smiled.

'You'd rather not tell me?'

'I don't remember what I was thinking.'

'You're a very poor liar. Your ears give you away because they wiggle.'

'Rubbish!'

'Was she blonde or brunette?'

'A redhead, with a body to make the Venus de Milo go on a crash diet.'

'No hands? What a pity. Cuts out so much of the fun . . . In fact, it wasn't a woman, was it? You were looking sad, not lustful. What's the trouble?' Her tone was no longer light and bantering; now it was soft and comforting. 'Were you mourning your lost principles?'

He looked at her with uneasy surprise.

She stood, crossed to his chair, kissed him. 'It's not a total disaster, you know. One good result is, it makes you more at one with the rest of us.'

'"Damn your principles! Stick to your party."?'

'Perhaps . . . Come on, love, let's move and go to bed.' She kissed him again.

He stood and reached out for the fire-guard to put in front of the fire which had burned low. He wondered how long it would be before he could stick to his party without any regrets.